THE BOBBSEY TWINS'
ADVENTURE IN WASHINGTON

The beautiful capital city of the United States is the scene of the exciting adventures of Bert, Nan, Freddie, and Flossie Bobbsey as they search for a Colonial china sugar bowl and creamer—not to mention the stolen blueprints of a space rider.

The twins, touring Washington, D. C., with their classmates, see all the famous landmarks. And everywhere they keep running into a strange character who sometimes wears a black beard and an Indian turban and sometimes appears dressed in ordinary American clothes. Flossie follows him into a foreign embassy, and you can imagine poor Nan's embarrassment when Freddie falls into the embassy pool during a party to which the Bobbseys haven't even been invited.

But Freddie's pranks are not always disastrous. When, sliding off the banister at the Supreme Court, he nearly knocks down "Mr. Justice," Freddie gets a special tour conducted by the famous judge himself. And it is Freddie who spots the "signal pole" that helps untangle the whole mystery of the missing space-rider plans.

THE BOBBSEY TWINS'
ADVENTURE IN WASHINGTON

Someone was running down the hillside!

The Bobbsey Twins' Adventure in Washington

By

LAURA LEE HOPE

GROSSET & DUNLAP
Publishers   *New York*

ISBN : 0–448–08012–5
PRINTED IN THE UNITED STATES OF AMERICA

The Bobbsey Twins' Adventure in Washington

CONTENTS

THE BOBBSEY TWINS'
ADVENTURE IN WASHINGTON

CHAPTER I

EXCITING PLANS

"BERT! You're going to the planet Mars!" exclaimed blond, six-year-old Flossie Bobbsey. She jumped up and down in excitement.

Her brother grinned. "But that's a long way from Pluto, the planet farthest from the earth."

"Now it's my turn!" cried Freddie, who was Flossie's twin.

Carefully he twirled the spinner in the center of the game board. Then he groaned. "I have to go back to earth!" He moved his paper disk to the starting point.

"Never mind, Freddie," said Nan Bobbsey comfortingly. "You'll catch up again." Nan was Bert's twin. They were twelve and had dark hair and eyes.

The four Bobbsey children were seated around the picnic table in the back yard of their home in Lakeport. They were playing with a new astronaut game their mother had just bought for them. Each hoped to win the game

1

and receive a prize Mrs. Bobbsey had offered.

At that moment a boy walked into the yard. He was about Bert's age but taller and heavier.

"Hello, Danny," Bert said coolly. He was never too glad to see Danny Rugg, who was a bully. He enjoyed playing mean tricks on the Bobbseys, particularly Freddie and Flossie.

Danny walked over to the table and sniffed. "What kind of stupid game is that?" he asked.

At the sound of Danny's voice, the Bobbseys' big white dog Snap got up from his place under the bushes and walked toward the group.

"It's an astronaut game," Nan explained. "You're supposed to try to get to the planet Pluto."

"I want to play, too." Danny put his elbows on the picnic table and leaned over the board.

"You'll have to wait until we finish this game," Freddie spoke up. "It's Flossie's turn to move."

"You kids make me sick! I don't want to play astronaut anyway!" Danny said rudely. With a swift movement of one hand he knocked over the spinner and scattered the paper disks.

Snap growled.

"That was a mean thing to do, Danny!" Bert protested. "You're just asking for trouble!"

Danny pulled back his arm as if to strike Bert. Before he could swing, Snap jumped on the bully, knocking him against the table.

"Hey! Call off your dog!" Danny yelled.

"Hey! Call off your dog!" Danny yelled.

"Down, Snap!" Nan ordered. The dog obediently dropped to the ground and went over to Nan. "You'd better leave, Danny."

"Okay! I'm going!" Danny glared at the twins. He turned and walked off down the driveway with Snap sniffing at his heels.

As Bert began to pick up the game, a plump, jolly-looking colored woman came out onto the back porch. "You children come in now and get ready for supper," she called. "Your daddy's bringing home company."

"Who is it, Dinah?" Flossie asked, running to the porch.

All the twins were very fond of Dinah Johnson, who had helped Mrs. Bobbsey with the housework ever since the twins could remember. She and her husband Sam, who worked in Mr. Bobbsey's lumberyard, had rooms on the third floor of the large rambling house.

"I don't know, honey child." Dinah ruffled the little girl's hair. "But your daddy will want you all to look spic 'n' span, so run upstairs and change your clothes."

When the children came downstairs they found their slender, pretty mother and tall, athletic father in the living room. With them was a middle-aged man. He was of medium height and had twinkling brown eyes.

"This is Mr. Ayler, children," Mr. Bobbsey

said. "He's—sort of a spacecraft engineer."

"Do you mean he drives around in space?" Freddie asked.

Mr. Ayler laughed. "Not yet," he replied. "But I'm working on an invention which will make it possible for a person to fly himself through space. I call it a space rider. I'm going to Washington soon to show it to some of the government authorities."

"Boy!" Bert exclaimed. "I'd certainly like to see that!"

"So would I!" Freddie cried, punching a sofa pillow.

"If you boys will stop at my factory some afternoon after school," Mr. Ayler suggested, "I'll show you a picture of it. I might even give you a toy rocket!"

Freddie let out a hoot. "That's great!"

The next morning on the way to school Bert and Freddie discussed when they would go to Mr. Ayler's factory. "I have baseball practice this afternoon and tomorrow," Bert said, "but I could go Thursday." So it was decided to pay the visit then.

When Bert and Nan entered their homeroom there was a buzz of conversation. Nellie Parks ran up to Nan. "I hear we might take a school trip to Washington D. C.!" she said excitedly. "Miss Vandermeer's going to tell us about it after the bell rings!"

Blond Nellie Parks was Nan's best friend. Bert's was Charlie Mason, tall and full of fun. The four children were in the same homeroom.

"A trip? Really?" cried Nan excitedly.

At the sound of the bell the children took their seats and the teacher stood behind her desk. Smiling, Miss Vandermeer announced that she and Mr. and Mrs. Tetlow, the principal and his wife, were planning to chaperon a bus trip to Washington D. C. for children from the two highest grades.

"We will leave a week from Saturday when the spring vacation begins and return the following Friday," she went on. "We would like to know by tomorrow how many of you can go. Talk to your parents." She handed out pamphlets giving the details.

"I hope Bert and I can make the trip," Nan said to Nellie as they left the building at noon.

"I'm pretty sure my mother and father will let me go," Nellie remarked. "Mother said the other day she wished I could see Washington soon."

"I'd like to go too," Charlie Mason said. Then he looked at Bert with a grin. "I heard Danny say he and Jack Westley were going!"

"Oh, no!" Bert groaned.

"We wouldn't have to pay any attention to them!" Nan said stoutly. "I still want to go!"

While the twins were eating lunch Bert told

their mother all about the proposed trip.

"It sounds wonderful," Mrs. Bobbsey agreed. "We'll talk to your father about it this evening."

"May Freddie and I go too?" Flossie asked.

Mrs. Bobbsey shook her head. "I'm afraid not, dear," she said. "The trip is just for the older children. But we'll think of something nice for you and Freddie to do."

Freddie looked unhappy. "Aw—bigger kids always get to do everything!" he groaned.

"You and Flossie will be older too some day," his mother said with a smile.

Just then Freddie noticed Dinah carrying in a large bowl of chocolate pudding for dessert, and he forgot his disappointment.

When Mr. Bobbsey heard the plan that evening, he agreed that Bert and Nan ought to make the trip.

"Oh, neat!" cried Bert.

"Thanks a lot." Nan hugged her father so hard he yelled, "Help!"

Mr. Bobbsey turned to Freddie and Flossie. "We'll cook up something special for my little fat fireman and my little fat fairy."

These were the nicknames that Mr. Bobbsey had given the plump younger twins. Ever since Freddie was a tiny boy he had been interested in being a fireman when he grew up.

Nan saw the sad look still on the younger twins' faces and hoped she could do something about it. The next morning she spoke to Miss Vandermeer about the Washington trip. The teacher said she would talk to the principal, but she was afraid that the younger children could not be included.

After school Mr. Tetlow stopped Nan as she was leaving the building. Chuckling, he said, "I have good news for you. We have two extra places in the bus. If your mother and father are willing, and you and Bert will promise to take care of Freddie and Flossie, they may come with us to Washington."

"Oh, thank you, Mr. Tetlow!" Nan said gratefully. "I'll speak to Mother and Dad and let you know."

When Freddie and Flossie heard the offer they were overjoyed. "Please, please, let us go!" Flossie pleaded. "We'll be very good—honest!"

"All right," Mrs. Bobbsey agreed, "but you must promise not to get into any mischief in Washington!"

"I'll see that they don't!" Bert said, pretending to look very stern.

Freddie and Flossie giggled, then began making plans about all the things they would do in the capital.

Freddie was waiting for Bert the next afternoon when he came out of school. "Remember, you and I are going to the space factory," he stated. "Mr. Ayler said he'd give us a rocket!"

"I hope you're not planning to take off in it!" Bert teased.

Freddie grinned and hurried along beside his brother. The factory was about half a mile from the school and it did not take the boys long to get there. The building was a large, low one set back in a grove of trees.

"I hope Mr. Ayler's here now," Bert remarked as they went up the walk.

When he spoke with the pretty receptionist, Miss Blake, she smiled at them. "Yes," she said, "Mr. Ayler is in. He told me you would be stopping by some afternoon. You can go to his office. It's back there."

She started to lead the way, but the telephone rang. "I'll have to answer this," Miss Blake explained, "but you can find your way. Just go in that door and through the drafting room. Mr. Ayler's office opens off the end of it."

Bert thanked her. Followed by Freddie, he pushed open the door to the drafting room. On the two long sides were windows. Under them stood four drawing tables.

The boys walked down the center aisle, looking interestedly from side to side. A tall young man came from Mr. Ayler's office at the end of the room, his arms full of dark blue papers.

"Come on, Freddie," Bert called as he reached the office. He looked back.

Freddie began to run, not looking where he

was going. *Crash!* He and the man collided with such force that the papers flew from his arms. They scattered on the floor.

"Oh, golly!" Freddie cried. "I'm sorry. I'll pick them all up."

"Never mind," the man said. He sounded annoyed. "I'll do it."

But Freddie bent over and picked up several of the drawings and handed them to the man. Then, still embarrassed, he ran to catch up to Bert.

"For Pete's sake, Freddie, watch where you're going!" his brother scolded. Then he knocked on the closed door.

"Come in!" a voice called.

They stepped into the room. Mr. Ayler looked up, nodded quickly, then resumed shuffling frantically among a pile of drawings on his desk.

"I can't find the blueprints of my invention!" he cried excitedly.

CHAPTER II

A CHINA MYSTERY

"YOUR space rider!" Bert cried. "You mean you lost the drawings of *that?*"

Mr. Ayler nodded and continued to turn over the papers on his desk. "They were here just a minute ago!" he muttered.

"What did they look like?" Freddie asked curiously.

"They were what we call blueprints, white lines on blue paper," the inventor replied. "One of them was a drawing of a man at the controls of the machine."

"I saw that!" Freddie said. "He was in a thing that looked sort of like a saucer! That man who just went out of here dropped the paper when I bumped into him. I picked it up and gave it back!"

"You *did?*" Mr. Ayler jumped up, threw open the door, and rushed out into the large room. In a few minutes he was back, several blueprints in his hands.

"That John Betz!" he said in disgust. "He's new here, and he's always making mistakes! It's a good thing you saw that drawing, Freddie. Betz says he thought the prints had been discarded and he was going to burn them!"

Mr. Ayler carefully put the drawings in the safe and spun the lock, then he turned to the boys. "Come, I'll show you around the plant," he said more calmly.

For a half hour Bert and Freddie watched tiny metal parts being stamped out by huge machines. Then in the assembly department they saw the parts put together to form pieces of equipment.

Finally they reached Mr. Ayler's office again. He went over to a shelf and took down a box containing two small plastic rockets. "I make these toys for some of my customers' children," he said with a smile. "Maybe you boys would enjoy playing with them. The directions are on the box."

"Thanks!" Bert exclaimed, pulling one out of its container. "They're sharp!"

Freddie's eyes lighted up. "This is neat, Mr. Ayler!"

While the boys were visiting the factory, Nan and Flossie had had an adventure of their own. Soon after they had returned from school, the telephone had rung.

Mrs. Bobbsey answered and the girls could

hear her say, "Yes, Miss Pompret, I'm sure Nan would be glad to take it for you."

When she hung up, the children's mother explained that their neighbor had asked if Nan would take a package to the post office for her. "She twisted her ankle and doesn't think she can walk that far."

"I'll go with you, Nan," Flossie volunteered, running to get her sweater. "I like Miss Pompret. She's pretty."

Miss Pompret had come to Lakeport a year or two before to work in the library. She had wavy brown hair and a friendly smile.

The young woman was waiting at the door when Nan and Flossie reached the small house where she lived. "You're sweet to do this for me," she said. "I want to send a birthday gift to my cousin in Washington and it's already late."

"We're going to Washington!" Flossie spoke up proudly. "Freddie and I are going with the big kids on the school bus!"

"That's lovely!" Miss Pompret said. "I used to live in Washington. If you'd like to stop in on your way back from the post office, I'll tell you about the exciting things you'll see there."

The girls promised and hurried off with the package. When they returned from their errand, Miss Pompret welcomed them.

"I baked a cake this morning," she said. "Won't you have some?"

"Oh, we always have room for cake," piped up Flossie.

The librarian led the girls into a small living room, then excused herself for a moment. Soon she returned with a tray on which were three glasses of milk, plates, and a big cake covered with fluffy white icing.

"Ooh!" Flossie exclaimed. "It looks yummy!"

While Miss Pompret served the cake, she told the girls that members of her family had lived in Washington for many years. "My grandmother owned a famous old house. Unfortunately she died a short while ago and the old house has been sold."

"That's too bad," Nan said sympathetically. "Mother says Washington is a beautiful city. It must have been nice to live—oh, Flossie!"

The little girl had taken too large a piece of cake onto her fork. It had fallen to the floor, squashy side down!

"I—I couldn't help it!" Flossie wailed.

"Now don't worry," said Miss Pompret. "No harm done. I'll cut you another piece."

Nan leaned down to pick up the cake, and wiped up most of the gooey mess. Miss Pompret hurried to get a wet cloth, and soon every bit of the spot was gone.

As Flossie apologized, Miss Pompret said laughingly, "Next time I bake a cake I won't make it so slippery."

"Package for Miss Pompret," the postman said.

She and the girls had just finished eating when the doorbell rang. Nan offered to answer it.

When she opened the door a postman stood there, a large box in his arms. "Package for Miss Pompret," he told her.

"Thank you," Nan said. She closed the door and carried the box to a table.

Miss Pompret examined the package. "This must be my grandmother's tea set!" she exclaimed happily. "She always said I was to have it!"

"I'll help you open the box," Nan said. She took some scissors from the desk and began to cut the twine which held the package.

When the box was open, she and Miss Pompret carefully lifted out the pieces of delicate bone china and set them on the table. There were four cups and saucers, four plates, and a graceful teapot. The china was cream-colored with dainty pink roses scattered over the surface.

"It's bee-yoo-ti-ful!" cried Flossie.

"And very old," Miss Pompret explained. "There is a legend in our family that George Washington's granddaughter, Nelly Custis, drank tea from these cups."

"How exciting!" Nan exclaimed as she bent to look more closely at the tea set.

"That's strange!" Miss Pompret said suddenly, examining the china pieces. "The cream pitcher and sugar bowl aren't here! Maybe they're still in the box."

"Oh, I hope so!" Nan exclaimed.

Miss Pompret and Nan felt carefully in the packing material left in the carton, but there was no more china.

"What could have happened to those pieces?" the librarian asked worriedly. "The last time I saw the tea set it was complete. I do hope the other pieces haven't been broken or lost!"

"We'll find them for you while we're in Washington," Flossie offered. "We love to look for lost things."

"That's sweet of you," Miss Pompret said gratefully. "And in the meantime, I'll try to get in touch with Grandmother's housekeeper and see if she knows anything about them."

Nan had been examining the teapot. "There's a mark at the bottom," she observed. "It looks like a lion in a circle."

"That's right, Nan. You'll find the same mark on the bottom of each piece. That's the trademark of the English maker. The same figure is on every piece of china made in his factory. In that way you can tell the original from a copy."

"Then all we have to do is look for a cream pitcher and sugar bowl with a lion on the bottom," Nan remarked eagerly.

As the girls got up to leave, Miss Pompret

said, "Have a nice time in Washington! It should be lovely this time of year when the cherry trees are in bloom."

Nan and Flossie thanked her for the cake and milk and hurried toward home, talking busily about the missing pieces of china. When they reached the house, they ran in to tell their family about it.

"Mother!" called Nan as she opened the door.

There was no answer until Dinah came in from the kitchen, her arms full of clothes. "Your mother went downtown," she told them. "I'm takin' these clothes up to the storage closet. They've been airin' all afternoon."

"Is Bert home yet?" Nan asked.

"He and Freddie are out in the yard," Dinah called back over her shoulder as she trudged up the stairs.

"Let's go tell them," Flossie suggested, running toward the kitchen.

But just at that moment the telephone rang. Nan answered. "Oh, yes, Mr. Ayler," she said. "No, Daddy's not home yet." She listened a few minutes, then said, "Yes, I'll tell him. We're going to Washington next week too, and we'll be staying at that same hotel."

Mr. Ayler said something, and Nan replied, "We'd love to! We'll be sure to look you up. Good-by."

"What did Mr. Ayler want?" Flossie called back from the kitchen door.

"He's going to Washington next week and wanted Daddy to know where he'd be. He wants us to have dinner with him there."

"Freddie and me too?" Flossie asked anxiously.

"Sure! He said all four of us twins."

Flossie smiled happily. "I'd better tell Freddie right away!" she announced.

When the two girls went out to the back yard they saw Bert and Freddie working with something at the picnic table.

Bert looked up. "Come on over here," he called. "See the rockets Mr. Ayler gave Freddie and me."

"They're great!" Freddie exclaimed. "You just put water in here and pump. Then you pull this little thing, and it blasts off!"

"Oh, let me try it!" Flossie begged.

While Freddie and Flossie were working with the toy rocket, Nan told Bert about Mr. Ayler's phone call.

"He said he was going to take the drawings of his invention to Washington," Bert reminded his twin. "It'll be fun to see him there."

"Watch, Nan! Watch the rocket!" Flossie cried. She closed her eyes and pulled the trigger. Nothing happened!

"It didn't go off!" Flossie said, and pouted a bit in disappointment.

Bert took the toy and worked with it a minute. "Now I think it's all right," he said, handing it back to Flossie.

Once more she pulled the trigger. The rocket did not move!

"I'll shoot it!" Bert took the rocket and began pumping vigorously.

"Now watch!" he said, taking a firm grip on the trigger and holding the toy away from him.

"Blast!" he yelled.

At that moment Dinah came out into the yard and walked toward some clothes hanging on the line. The rocket took off with a *swish* and headed straight for her!

CHAPTER III

THE FROG JOKE

"LOOK out, Dinah!" Flossie shrieked. "The rocket's coming!"

At Flossie's cry the cook ducked her head. The toy rocket soared above her harmlessly!

"My goodness!" Dinah scolded, frowning. "What you tryin' to do to old Dinah?"

"I'm sorry," Bert said. "Something went wrong. The rocket was supposed to go straight up in the air!"

The frown left Dinah's face. "All right, Bert," she said. "There's no harm done, but don't you go shootin' any more of those things at me!"

"Maybe you should leave the rocket on the table so it'll go straight up," Nan suggested.

"How'd you all like some cookies?" Dinah asked, to make Bert feel better. "If you do, come on into the kitchen."

The mention of food made Nan think of the cake at Miss Pompret's house. "Flossie and I found a mystery—I almost forgot!" she said, as they all settled around the big kitchen table.

"Hey, what kind of mystery?" Freddie wanted to know.

"A cream pitcher mystery!" Flossie replied mischievously.

Freddie and Bert looked disgusted, but when their sisters told them the story of Miss Pompret's missing bone china, they were interested.

"It will be great to have something to look for in Washington," Bert agreed. "We haven't solved a mystery in a long time!"

The next week was a busy one for the twins. Homework had to be finished before Saturday when the bus would leave for Washington. Nan and Flossie helped their mother get the children's clothes ready for the trip.

At a meeting of the pupils making the trip Mr. Tetlow announced, "Each of you will write an essay on his most interesting experience in the capital, so keep your eyes open!"

"I didn't know we'd have to work on this trip!" Charlie Mason remarked to Bert.

"It shouldn't be too hard. Five days in Washington—something's *bound* to happen!" Bert reassured his friend.

Friday evening Miss Pompret called the Bobbseys to wish them a good trip. "I wrote my grandmother's housekeeper about the missing pieces of china," she told Nan, "but my letter was returned. The postman wrote on it that she's no longer at that address."

"We can't wait to search for the sugar bowl and creamer," Nan replied.

"If you have an opportunity, perhaps you can go out to the old house and look around," Miss Pompret said. "It's in the Georgetown section of Washington."

Nan carefully wrote down the address and put the slip of paper in her purse. "We'll let you know, Miss Pompret."

Early the next morning the bus stopped in front of the Bobbsey home. Miss Vandermeer helped the twins get settled in their seats. Then with much waving they were off.

Mr. and Mrs. Tetlow had taken seats in the rear of the bus, while Miss Vandermeer sat toward the front. Danny Rugg and Jack Westley were seated directly in front of Freddie and Flossie.

For a while all the children enjoyed pushing and releasing the buttons on the arms of each seat to make the backs lower or raise.

As the bus passed Lake Metoka, on its way to the main road, the driver slowed. "I'm going to stop here, folks, for a few minutes. I want to shift the baggage."

He jumped out and opened the storage compartment under the bus. Then he began to rearrange the suitcases. Some of the children got out and walked to the edge of the lake.

"Okay, everyone, back in the bus!" Mr. Tetlow called later. "We're ready to leave!"

As Freddie and Flossie started back, Freddie suddenly stopped and picked up something.

"What's that?" Flossie wanted to know.

"Ssh! I'll tell you later."

When they were in their seats once more, Freddie cautiously opened his hand and showed Flossie what was in it.

"Oh! A baby frog!" Flossie squealed. "Are you going to take him to Washington?"

Freddie nodded with an impish look, then glanced around for some place to put his treasure. The little boy's eyes spotted the ash tray which was fastened to the back of the seat in front of him. Quickly he raised the top and slid the little frog into the metal container.

Flossie giggled. "That's a neat place!"

The bus turned onto the highway and picked up speed. Someone started a song and soon everyone was singing gaily.

The time seemed to pass quickly, but just before noon Danny and Jack began wrestling. The seat shook as the two boys bounced around. Then Jack's hand hit the button which controlled the back of the seat.

Bang! It fell down. The sudden motion caused the ash receiver to flip open. *Freddie's frog tumbled out!*

"Catch him!" Flossie shrieked.

But it was too late. The little frog leaped down the aisle. Miss Vandermeer had put her handbag on the floor beside her seat. The escaping frog landed on it.

Freddie crept forward, his hand outstretched to grab the animal. But just as he reached to capture it, the frog leaped again. This time he landed in Miss Vandermeer's lap.

"Oh!" she screamed.

All the children jumped to their feet and peered to see what had happened. A wave of laughter swept over the bus as Freddie, his face red, finally picked up the frog.

Freddie gulped. "I'm sorry he scared you, Miss Vandermeer. But he won't hurt you."

The teacher laughed. "I know that, Freddie," she said kindly, "but he *did* startle me!"

By this time Bert had reached his brother. "You'll have to let the frog go," he decided.

Miss Vandermeer took a large envelope from her purse. "If Freddie wants to keep him in this for a while, perhaps we can find something better when we stop for lunch," she said, seeing the little boy's disappointed expression.

"Thanks, Miss Vandermeer!" Freddie beamed as he slipped his pet into the envelope and went back to his seat.

A short time later the bus pulled up at a restaurant and the children piled out. When the

"Oh!" screamed Miss Vandermeer.

teacher explained Freddie's problem to one of the waiters he smiled, nodded, and went off.

Presently he came back with a round coffee can with holes punched in the top. The waiter had even placed some wet leaves in the bottom.

"That's great! Thank you!" said Freddie.

The man laughed. "I have a little boy of my own who likes frogs," he said.

Freddie took the frog from the envelope and put it into the can. He kept the can beside him while he ate his lunch and carefully put it on the bus seat for the rest of the day.

Late that afternoon the driver stopped at an attractive motor lodge. The children were assigned to rooms, and later met in the motel's restaurant for supper. After that they watched a television program in the lounge, then made their way sleepily back to their rooms.

Freddie, who was sharing one with Bert, ran at once to look at his frog. He took the lid from the coffee can and gave a gasp.

"He's gone, Bert! My frog's gone!"

Bert came to look. "But how could he get out of the can?" he asked in bewilderment. "Was he in there when you went to supper?"

Freddie nodded vigorously.

"Well, we can't do anything about it now," Bert said with a yawn. "Maybe he'll turn up in the morning."

While Freddie stared mournfully at the

empty coffee can, Bert put on his pajamas and slipped into bed. The next minute a queer expression came over his face.

"Freddie," he called, "I think I know where your frog is!"

"Where?" his brother asked eagerly.

"In my bed!"

Freddie ran across the room as Bert carefully pulled down the bed covers. The little frog was crouched near the bottom. Before he could leap out, Freddie cupped him in his hands and dropped him into the coffee can.

"How do you s'pose he got in your bed, Bert?" Freddie asked, puzzled.

"I have a good idea!" said Bert grimly. "But I think I'll just let the one who put him there wonder about it until morning!"

"You mean Danny?"

"I wouldn't put it past him!"

With the frog safe in his new home, the two boys soon fell asleep.

When they went into the dining room the next morning, Danny eyed them cheerily. "Have a good sleep, Bert?" he asked.

"Sure, Danny. You thought you were pretty smart slipping that frog in my bed, didn't you?"

Danny put on an air of injured innocence. "What are you talking about?"

"So that was what you were doing!" Charlie

Mason said. "I saw you leave the lounge while we were watching television!"

"Okay, so what if I *did* put the frog in your bed?" Danny blustered. "Can't you take a joke?"

"Sure, *I* can," Bert said, "but I don't think the frog liked it very much!"

Later when the baggage was being packed into the bus, Flossie ran up to Freddie. "I met a little girl in the lobby," she said. "She lives in the motel, and she'd like to have your frog if you want to leave it here."

Freddie looked doubtful. Then he held out the coffee can to Flossie. "All right," he decided. "I s'pose I can't keep him forever. You can give him to her. Maybe he wouldn't like it in Washington anyway!"

The day's ride was fun, and late in the afternoon the bus reached Washington. The sun was low in the sky and the white stone of the big government buildings glowed in its light.

"It's bee-yoo-ti-ful!" Flossie cried as they drove down a broad avenue lined with flowering trees. A few minutes later the bus drew up in front of their hotel.

"Let's go see Mr. Ayler as soon as we can," Nan suggested to Bert.

"Okay," he agreed. "Freddie and I'll meet you and Flossie in the lobby."

When the girls came down fifteen minutes

later, the boys were already there. "I asked the desk clerk," Bert announced. "Mr. Ayler's in room six-oh-four. Let's go see him."

They rode up in the elevator and hurried along the hall peering at the door numbers.

Finally Freddie stopped. "Here it is—six-oh-four!" he called to the others.

As Bert started to knock, he paused. "What's that queer noise?" he asked in surprise, putting his ear closer to the door. The noise came again, still louder.

"Someone's groaning!" Nan cried. "Open the door, Bert, if you can! Quick!"

CHAPTER IV

BANISTER EXPRESS

BERT lost no time. He pushed open the unlocked door. The twins stared in amazement. Tied to a chair, with a gag in his mouth, was the inventor!

"Mr. Ayler!" Nan brushed past Bert and ran to the chair. "Are you hurt?" Quickly she pulled the rolled-up hand towel from his mouth while Bert took out his pocketknife and cut the rope which bound the man.

Mr. Ayler stood up and stretched his arms. "Thank goodness you children came!" he said gratefully. "I might have been here all night without anyone finding me!"

"Grasshoppers! What happened?" Freddie asked excitedly. "Who tied you up?"

"I must call the police, then I'll tell you all about it," Mr. Ayler said, picking up the telephone. "The plans of my invention have been stolen!"

"Oh, no!" cried Nan.

"How terrible!" Bert exclaimed.

After Mr. Ayler had made his report to the police, he turned back to the four children. "An officer is coming right over," he said, "but in the meantime I'll tell you what happened."

The inventor explained that several hours earlier he had answered a knock on his door. Two masked men had forced themselves in. Before Mr. Ayler could recover from his surprise, they had tied him to the chair and thrust the gag into his mouth. They had then left, taking his attaché case which contained the drawings.

"Didn't you see what they looked like?" Nan asked.

"They were both masked," the inventor replied, "but while I was struggling to keep from being tied to the chair, one of the men's masks slipped a bit. I saw that he had a square-cut black beard!"

"Are the men tall or short?" Bert questioned.

"They're both of medium height, but the one whose face I *didn't* see is stockier than the other. And I've just remembered something! The bearded man had a star-shaped scar on the back of his left hand!"

At this moment there was a knock on the door. Bert opened it and two plain-clothes men walked in. They introduced themselves as Dan Hogan and Harry Roth.

"If you'll give us the details of this robbery,"

Mr. Hogan said, "we'll do our best to find your property for you."

Once more Mr. Ayler went through the account of what had happened that afternoon. The detective wrote it all in a little notebook.

When the inventor told of the missing attaché case, Mr. Hogan looked up. "What color was the case? Did it have any marks on it?" he asked.

"It was black, and in one corner it had my initials in gold," was the reply.

The police officer closed his book and stood up. "We'll keep in touch with you, Mr. Ayler," he promised, "and if we find any clues we'll let you know."

Freddie announced, "We'll look for clues too. We're good detectives!"

"Is that so?" Mr. Hogan smiled. "Well, we're always glad to have all the help we can get. If you learn any information, call us at headquarters."

The officers left and Mr. Ayler thanked the twins again for having come to his rescue. "I'll probably be in Washington for a week or so. We'll have dinner together some night."

The children said good-by and went down to the lobby again. As they reached it, Bert said, "I have an idea! Wait here."

Nan stood with the younger twins at the postcard stand while Bert walked out the front door.

She could see him speaking to the doorman.

In a few minutes he was back. "What were you talking about?" Flossie wanted to know.

Bert was excited. "I asked that man at the door if he had noticed anyone leaving here this afternoon with a black attaché case."

"Had he?" asked Nan.

"Yes. He says two men hurried away together. One had a black beard. The other was smooth shaven. He was carrying a black case!"

"Did he see where they went?"

"They got into a black Ronda and drove away."

"What's a Ronda?" Flossie inquired.

"It's a foreign car," Bert explained. "Maybe those men were spies!"

"Spies!" Freddie's eyes opened wide. "We have to find them!"

"Don't you think you'd better call Mr. Hogan and tell him about the car?" Nan suggested.

When Bert spoke to police headquarters, he learned that the detectives had just returned from the hotel.

"Good for you, Bert!" Mr. Hogan said. "That's a big help. Did the doorman by any chance get the license number?"

"Hold on and I'll find out," Bert replied. When he came back he told the officer that the doorman had noticed only that the license plate was from the District of Columbia.

"Well, that narrows it down a bit," Hogan said. "The driver evidently lives in Washington and not in any of the Virginia or Maryland suburbs. We'll concentrate our search here."

As the twins stood talking by the telephone, Nellie Parks came in search of them. "Where have you all been?" she asked. "Mr. Tetlow is taking us to a travel movie after dinner and we've been looking for you."

Nan explained about the theft of Mr. Ayler's drawings and their efforts to catch the men.

"I knew you Bobbseys would find a mystery in Washington!" Nellie commented with a laugh. "Forget it for now and let's meet everyone for dinner and the movie."

The picture was a thrilling one about the wild animal parks in Africa, and all the children enjoyed it. When they parted for the night, Miss Vandermeer reminded them that the sightseeing trip would start after breakfast the next day.

The bus was waiting as they came out of the hotel in the morning. "Our first stop will be at the Supreme Court Building," Mr. Tetlow announced when the big vehicle got under way.

It was a bright, clear day and the white columns of the building were dazzling in the morning sun. The school children eagerly climbed the long flight of steps to the entrance.

Inside, Mr. Tetlow led them through the

wide marble hall to the courtroom at the rear.
There he pointed out the chairs of the Justices
behind the long table.

"The chairs are all different!" Nan exclaimed
in surprise.

"Yes," Mr. Tetlow explained. "Each Justice
has his own chair and he picks one which is
most comfortable for him!"

As the school principal continued to talk
about the Supreme Court, Danny Rugg edged
over until he was standing next to Freddie.
"There's a neat stairway down that hall," he
whispered. "Have you seen it?"

Freddie shook his head.

"Come on and I'll show it to you!"

Freddie could not understand very much of
what Mr. Tetlow was saying, so he decided to
go with Danny. They walked down a hall opening off the central one, then turned a corner.

"See! Isn't that neat?" Danny pointed out a
marble spiral stairway which wound from the
basement up to the third floor. It had a polished
bronze banister.

"I've counted seven spirals," Danny informed
Freddie, "two for each floor and one for the
basement. It'd be great to slide down, but of
course you couldn't do it. You're too young."

"Why not?" Freddie asked.

"Aw! You'd be scared!"

"I would not!"

"Okay. Go ahead then. I dare you!"

Freddie could not resist. He ducked under the chain which blocked off the stairway and climbed onto the banister. The next minute he was whizzing downward! Danny ran away.

The turns came so fast that Freddie quickly grew dizzy. But he clung to the smooth bronze banister until he reached the bottom. By that time he was going too fast to stop. He shot off the banister right into a dignified-looking man! The little boy nearly knocked him over.

"Bless my soul!" the man exclaimed. "What's this?"

Freddie scrambled to his feet. "I'm sorry," he stammered. "I couldn't stop."

The man laughed. "I guess I'd have done the same thing when I was your age. That stairway is mighty tempting!"

"Where am I, sir?" Freddie asked. "I think I'm lost!"

"You're in the basement of the building," his new friend explained. "This door leads out to the parking lot. But if you'd like to come up in the elevator with me, I'll show you some pictures."

Freddie followed the man into the elevator and out onto the main floor. A guard standing nearby respectfully touched his cap and said, "Good morning, Mr. Justice."

"Is your name Justice?" Freddie asked.

The man laughed. "Well, a lot of people call me that!"

"My name's Freddie!" the little boy said proudly.

The man smiled warmly and led Freddie into a room where the walls were lined with pictures of men in black robes.

"There are some very famous men here," the stranger said. "They are former Justices of the Supreme Court."

Freddie walked around and peered up at the pictures. "They look very smart," he observed politely.

At that moment Mr. Tetlow appeared in the doorway. "So, there you are, Freddie," he called rather sternly. "We're ready to leave now."

Freddie walked over to the school principal. "This is Mr. Justice," he explained. "He was showing me some pictures."

"Good morning, sir," Mr. Tetlow said. "I hope this young man hasn't been bothering you."

"On the contrary," the man said, "I've enjoyed meeting him."

Freddie waved good-by and followed Mr. Tetlow to the bus. "He was a nice man, wasn't he?" he said.

"Yes, he's one of the greatest judges in the history of the Supreme Court," Mr. Tetlow said with a smile. "You had an important

It was a black Ronda!

guide!" Freddie's mouth dropped open in astonishment.

The other children were in the bus, but Bert stood outside waiting for his small brother. "Freddie, you stay with me or Nan," he said. "Mr. Tetlow had to look all over for you!"

As Bert started to step into the bus, he glanced at a car passing close by. It was a black Ronda!

"Say," Bert cried out, "that's the car we're looking for!"

As the automobile sped on, he dashed up the street in pursuit. When the Ronda reached the corner, the light turned red, and the driver stopped. Bert crossed with the green light and ran up to the window on the driver's side.

"Were—" he began, then stopped. The driver was a dark-complexioned man with a black beard, and wore a bright pink turban. He stared at Bert haughtily.

"I'm sorry!" the boy stammered. "I thought you were someone else!"

At that moment the light began to change. Bert hurried to the curb, but his eyes remained on the man. Suddenly he noticed the driver's hands. On the back of the left one was a star-shaped scar!

CHAPTER V

DANNY IS STUNG

A STAR-shaped scar! Mr. Ayler had seen just such a mark on the hand of the man who had stolen his space rider plans! Quickly Bert pulled a pad from his pocket and wrote down the car's license number.

"Come on, Bert," Charlie Mason called, leaning out of the bus window, "you're holding everybody up!"

Bert slid into the seat beside Charlie and told him about the man in the foreign car.

"Do you really think he was the thief?" Charlie asked in an excited tone.

"He could be. Anyway, as soon as we get back to the hotel I'm going to call the police and give them that license number!"

"We'll have a short drive around the city before going back to the hotel," Mr. Tetlow announced from his seat in the front of the bus.

41

They swung around the huge Capitol Building with its big round cupola and down Independence Avenue to the Tidal Basin and the Jefferson Memorial. Mr. Tetlow told the children that the flowering cherry trees which lined the pond had been presented to the city of Washington many years before by the city of Tokyo, Japan.

"They're bee-yoo-ti-ful!" Flossie sighed.

"As you can see, many people come to Washington each spring to see them." Mr. Tetlow pointed out the long line of cars driving slowly through the park.

Above the trees ahead, the children could see the round, white marble structure with its dignified columns built as a memorial to Thomas Jefferson, the third President of the United States. The bus drove on through the park along the Potomac River and past the memorial to President Lincoln, then to the hotel.

From his room Bert called Detective Hogan and reported the license number on the black Ronda. "And the driver had a star-shaped scar on his left hand."

The officer was surprised when Bert mentioned that the driver was wearing a pink turban.

"Sounds like an East Indian," he said. "You must have the wrong car. But we'll check it anyway and let you know what we find out."

Bert thanked the detective and went down to the dining room to join the others for an early lunch. Afterward, the travelers were driven to the Smithsonian Institution. On the way, Mr. Tetlow explained that the money to found the Institution had been left by an Englishman, James Smithson, who had never been in the United States!

"That was over a hundred years ago," the principal continued. "Since then this huge museum has grown tremendously and is a place where men may learn more about the world they live in."

When the children piled out of the bus and entered the Arts and Industry Building, the first things they saw were several strange-looking airplanes suspended from the ceiling.

"Look at that one!" Freddie cried. "The pilot is lying down to fly the plane!"

He pointed to an aircraft with two wings, one above the other, which seemed to be made of thin cloth. Stretched out on the lower wing was the dummy figure of a man.

"That's supposed to be Orville Wright. His was the first airplane to fly," Miss Vandermeer told the pupils. "It was built in 1903 and on its original flight stayed in the air for only twelve seconds!"

"I don't see how it stayed up *that* long," Bert remarked with a grin.

"And look at this one!" Charlie called. It was slightly more substantial, a single-winged craft with a small cabin.

"This is the plane Charles Lindbergh flew alone across the ocean to Paris in 1927," Bert read from the sign on the side of the aircraft.

While the boys continued to examine the old planes, Nan and Nellie walked over to look at an exhibition of dresses which had been worn by various Presidents' wives. The girls were delighted by the different styles, and especially liked the very fancy dresses of lovely lace-trimmed silks and satins.

Flossie had run ahead into another room. Now she came back and took Nan's hand. "Come and see the doll house!" she cried. "It has two sets of twins in it!"

Nan and Nellie followed the little girl until they came to a large glass case. Ten miniature rooms of the house were displayed inside. The sign explained that this was supposed to be the home of Peter Doll, his wife, and their six children in the early part of the twentieth century.

"See!" Flossie cried, pointing to two tiny figures in a nursery. "There are the baby twins, Jimmy and Timmy! And down here having a tea party are Carol and Lucy. They're twins too!"

"Aren't they darling!" Nan exclaimed. "I

wonder if they had as much fun together as *we* do!"

While the girls were admiring the doll house, the boys went up onto the balcony. This surrounded a rotunda in the middle of the building.

"Hey! Look at this, Charlie!" Bert called.

In a secluded corner he had come across a beehive. It was made of glass framed in wood, and the swarm of bees was plainly visible.

Charlie ran up, and the two boys peered at the busy bees. "Look! It opens to the outside of the building!" Charlie cried. Running from the main hive was a small glass-covered corridor. The end of this was an opening in the outside wall. Bees flew in and out.

"What are you looking at?" Danny Rugg came up and leaned his elbows on the glass cover. "Say! Look at those crazy bees!"

"Be careful, Danny," Bert warned. "That sign says not to lean on the case."

"Aw! I'm not hurting anything!" Danny sneered.

At that moment there came a loud *crack*. The top piece of glass broke into several parts! A number of bees flew into the room through the opening.

"Ouch!" Danny yelled and clapped his hand to his forehead. "I've been stung!"

"Ouch!" Danny yelled. "I've been stung!"

The boy's shouts brought a guard running. When he saw what had happened, the man quickly went for a length of cardboard and put it over the top of the glass compartment. Then he carefully chased the loose bees under the cover and taped it down.

"I hope that will last until I can get some new glass," he observed. "Can't you boys read the sign?"

Danny had run off, nursing his bee sting. Bert and Charlie apologized for him and told the guard they were sorry for the trouble he had caused.

In the meantime Freddie and some of the other children had gone to another building to see the air and space displays. They saw the Freedom 7, the first manned spacecraft to fly around the earth, and Freddie chuckled at the other models containing the monkeys, Able and Baker, in their nose cones.

As Freddie wandered about among the space exhibits he noticed a young man busily sketching an airplane motor. "Maybe he's a spy!" Freddie thought excitedly. "I'll get a guard!"

A good-natured attendant walked toward the young man, whom Freddie pointed out, and asked him a few questions. "He's an engineering student," the guard told the little boy when he came back. "Lots of students come here to sketch the motors. They're not spies!"

By this time the girls had examined all the little rooms in the doll house. They strolled out into the rotunda where the giant Statue of Freedom stood in the center.

Miss Vandermeer came up to them. "This is a duplicate of the figure which is on top of the Capitol dome," she said.

"Miss Freedom looks awf'ly fat!" Flossie observed.

The teacher laughed. "Maybe that's so she won't blow away in the wind!" Miss Vandermeer suggested teasingly, and Flossie giggled.

"I see some china up there on the balcony," Nan remarked to her sister when the teacher had wandered away. "Let's go and look at it."

"All right," Flossie agreed. "Maybe Miss Pompret's cream pitcher and sugar bowl are there!"

The girls climbed the stairs and walked slowly through the exhibit, admiring the display of old china. But there were no pieces which resembled Miss Pompret's china.

Finally Flossie began to droop. "I'm tired!" she complained. "Can't we sit down?"

"I'm tired too," Nan admitted. "I saw some benches out in front of the building. Let's sit there until the others come out."

When Nan and Flossie reached the benches, several of them were occupied by grownups enjoying the warm spring sun. The girls found places on a bench in front of a hedge.

"I like Washington, don't you?" Flossie remarked, swinging her legs contentedly.

"Yes, I do," Nan agreed, "and I hope we can find Mr. Ayler's plans and Miss Pompret's china while we're here."

Nan and Flossie were discussing the mysteries when they noticed a young woman and a little boy of about four sit down on a bench across the walk from them. The woman looked very tired.

"But, Mommy, I want to play ball!" the little boy said.

"Play by yourself for a while, Timmy," his mother begged.

"But I want to play with someone!" the child insisted.

Flossie called over to him. "I'll play with you! Throw your ball to me."

Timmy beamed. "Okay," he said. "I'll throw, and you catch!"

He tossed the ball, but it did not land very near Flossie. She got up and ran after it, then threw the ball back to Timmy. The game went on in this way for some time. Suddenly the little boy threw the ball very hard. It hit the edge of one bench, bounced across the path, and rolled under the seat where Nan was.

"My ball's gone!" Timmy looked as if he were about to cry.

"I'll get it for you," Flossie assured him. "Don't cry!"

She crawled under the bench and in a minute the red ball rolled out onto the path again. "There's something else under here," Flossie called. "I'll get it!"

There were sounds of tugging, then Flossie backed out from under the bench, a black attaché case in her hand.

Nan reached to take it from her. The next moment she gave a startled cry. "Look!" she said. "The case has Mr. Ayler's initials on it!"

CHAPTER VI

A FINGERPRINT CLUE

"MR. AYLER'S?" Flossie exclaimed. "Then I've found the case the men stole from him! Let's see if the plans are in it!"

Hurriedly Nan opened the attaché case. It was empty. "The thief wouldn't leave the drawings in here," she said. Then, seeing Flossie's disappointment, she added quickly, "But it's a wonderful clue!"

By this time the other children were beginning to assemble at the bus. Nan and Flossie waved good-by to the little boy and his mother and ran up to Bert and Freddie.

"Look what I found!" Flossie cried, waving the black case.

Bert took it from her. "Mr. Ayler's!" he said in amazement. "Where did you get it?"

Flossie told him it had been wedged between the back leg of the bench and the bottom of the hedge. "I never would have found it 'cept I

51

crawled under there to get a little boy's ball!"

"This is great!" Bert said excitedly. "We ought to take it to the police right away!"

At this moment Miss Vandermeer walked up to the twins. "What's the matter?" she asked. "You seem upset."

Bert and Nan told her the whole story of Mr. Ayler's invention and the theft of his drawings. "We think we should take this case to the police," Bert concluded.

"I think so, too," Miss Vandermeer agreed. She hesitated a moment, then said, "If you like, I'll take you there in a taxi. We can meet the others at the Justice Department Building, which is the next stop on our tour."

"Oh, thank you!" Nan said gratefully.

Miss Vandermeer explained the situation to Mr. Tetlow, then climbed into a taxi with the twins.

Mr. Hogan was in his office and greeted the children warmly. "What have my assistants found now?" he asked with a smile.

When Flossie showed him the attaché case with the initials in the corner, his jaw dropped. "Where on earth did you get this?" he cried.

Flossie described the hiding place outside the Smithsonian Institution.

"The thief probably went into the Air and Space Building to study some of the exhibits," Mr. Hogan guessed, "and decided to get rid of

the case there. This could be a big break for us,"
he went on happily. "I'll have it examined for
fingerprints and let you know the result."

"We're going to the Department of Justice
now," Nan spoke up, "but we'll probably go
back to the hotel after that."

"I'll call you," the detective promised as they
left his office.

When Miss Vandermeer and the twins
reached the Justice Department, the school
group was just arriving. They were waiting for
a guide to take them on a tour of the Federal
Bureau of Investigation.

A few minutes later a young man came up to
Mr. Tetlow. "Is Bert Bobbsey with your
group?" he asked.

"Right here!" Bert called out.

"I'm Jim Haley," the young man introduced
himself. "I'm to be your guide through the
F.B.I. But first I have a message for Bert."

"For me?" Bert asked in surprise.

"Yes. Mr. Hogan wants me to tell you that
the fingerprints on that attaché case you left
with him belong to a man named Henry Kraus."

"He's found out already?" Nan asked in
amazement.

"Yes, he sent the prints over for us to check.
We have millions of fingerprints on file at our
F.B.I.," Mr. Haley said proudly, "but it takes
us only six minutes to identify a set if it's here.

In this case it was easy because that thief is a former government employee and we have all such prints on file.

"Oh, I forgot to tell you," Mr. Haley went on, "Mr. Hogan says that license number you gave him is registered in Kraus's name. The District of Columbia police will start a search and pick him up for questioning."

"I thought we were going to see the F.B.I!" Danny Rugg called out rudely, "not solve Bert Bobbsey's silly mystery!"

"Just follow me," the guide said politely, "and I'll show you some of our laboratories."

He led the way to an elevator, and they rode up. The children stepped off on an upper floor with the adults and walked along several corridors. As the children peered through the glass partitions, which revealed the open labs, Jim Haley explained what the men in the rooms were doing. "These scientists of the Bureau can establish many facts by examining a few strands of hair or even threads of a cloth. From a tiny dot of paint they can tell the make and model of the car it was on. The automobile manufacturers send us samples of all the paints they use, and they're kept on file here."

He took the visitors back downstairs. Mr. Haley showed them photographs of the ten most wanted men in the country. "If you see one of these men, call your nearest F.B.I. office," he urged.

"Let's look for them, Flossie," Freddie suggested.

When there was no reply he looked around the group. The little girl was not there!

Flossie, meanwhile, had lagged behind as the group reached the first floor. Seeing a large courtyard through one of the long windows, she stopped to look out. On a raised space in the middle of the court was a fountain. Around it were tables and chairs and brightly colored umbrellas.

"That's pretty!" thought Flossie. "I wish we could go out there."

At that moment she felt something cold against her hand. She looked down. Beside her stood a big brown dog wagging his tail in friendly fashion.

"Hello," Flossie said, leaning over to pat the animal. "What's your name?"

The dog bounded down the hall, then stopped and looked back at Flossie. He seemed to want to play. As Flossie ran toward him, a young woman came from a nearby office. "Is this your dog?" the little girl asked her.

"No. You'd better take him outside. Dogs aren't allowed in here." She hurried around a corner and disappeared.

"You're not my dog," Flossie said.

"You're not my dog either," Flossie said to the animal, "but you look nice. I'll take you out to that fountain."

The dog followed happily as Flossie found an exit and went out into the courtyard. There they raced up and down until both were panting.

As Flossie flopped down into one of the chairs near the fountain, a man ran out from the building. "Here, Brownie!" he called. The dog dashed over to him.

The man threw out a ball, which the dog scooped up, balancing it on his nose. Flossie giggled in delight.

The man walked over to the fountain. "Hello there," he said to Flossie. "Have you been taking care of Brownie? He was tied up in my office, but got loose and ran away."

"I was just playing with him," Flossie replied. "He was lonesome."

"I was keeping him until my wife could come for him," the man explained. "She's here now. If you'll wait a second, I'll take him to her. Then I'll bring you a cold drink."

Flossie nodded. In a few minutes the man was back with a tall paper cup of cherry soda. "There you are," he said cheerily. "And thanks for taking care of Brownie."

Flossie was sitting by the fountain sipping her soda when Nan ran out into the courtyard. "Flossie! You know you're supposed to stay with me!" her sister said sternly. "We were all ready to leave, and no one could find you!"

"I'm sorry, Nan," the little girl said. "I just stopped for a minute, and then Brownie came along!" She told her sister about the dog and his nice master.

"I'm glad you had a good time, but we'll have to hurry. The bus is waiting for us!"

During the ride back to the hotel, Nan and Flossie sat across the aisle from Miss Vandermeer. "You've made a lot of progress toward solving your mystery today, haven't you?" the teacher said with a smile.

"We have *two* mysteries!" Flossie piped up.

"You have? What is the other one?"

Flossie told Miss Vandermeer the story of Miss Pompret's missing cream pitcher and sugar bowl.

"We have the address of her grandmother's house," Nan remarked. "We'd like to go out there and see if we can find the china."

"Where is the house?" Miss Vandermeer asked.

Nan took the slip of paper with the address on it from her purse. The teacher read it. "This is in Georgetown. It's a very old part of Washington. In fact, it was a town before the capital city was built."

"How can we get there?" Nan asked.

"I think you can get a bus near the hotel

which will take you very close to this street,"
Miss Vandermeer replied. "Would you like me
to go out there with you this afternoon?"

"Oh, will you?" Nan said gratefully. "That'll
be wonderful."

Nan called to Bert and Freddie when the bus
arrived at the hotel. She told them that Miss
Vandermeer would take them to Georgetown.

"You and Flossie go on," Bert suggested. "I
want to talk to Mr. Ayler and Freddie can come
with me. We'll see you later."

"Okay," Nan agreed.

As Miss Vandermeer had thought, they found
a bus near the hotel which would take them to
Georgetown. The ride seemed short because
there were so many interesting things to watch
from the windows.

Finally Miss Vandermeer reached up and
rang the buzzer to signal the driver to stop.
When she and the twins got off they stood on the
corner and looked around. Many of the houses
were tall and narrow and built close to the side-
walks. In the yards and along the street were
pretty flowering trees.

"It's lovely!" Nan exclaimed.

"Many well-known people live in this section," Miss Vandermeer told the girls. "Most of
these houses are over a hundred years old, but
they have been changed inside and are very
modern."

"Which one is Miss Pompret's grandmother's house?" Flossie asked.

"I think it must be on the next street," the teacher said. "I'll ask this man."

She spoke to a passerby and showed him the address. He pointed across the cobblestone street and motioned to his left. She thanked him and turned back to the girls.

"It's just about a block from here," she reported. "Come on."

The three followed the man's directions and in a few minutes stopped before an old red-brick house. A short flight of steps bordered by iron railings led up to the white door. The windows were uncurtained, and the house seemed deserted.

Nan rang the bell and waited. There was no answer.

CHAPTER VII

A SUBWAY CHASE

"WHAT shall we do?" Nan asked when no one came to the door. "The house seems to be empty."

"Let's peek inside," Flossie suggested.

She walked across the narrow strip of grass between the house and the sidewalk. Then, standing on tiptoe, she peered through the low window.

Nan ran down the steps and stood next to Flossie, shading her eyes to see inside. "There's still some furniture there," she observed. "It's covered up with sheets."

"Perhaps someone is working here but has left for the day," Miss Vandermeer guessed. "It is a little late. You might try to telephone the house tomorrow morning before we start out for our sightseeing. Maybe you'll be able to reach someone then."

The girls were disappointed at not finding anyone at the house but agreed there was nothing more they could do at the moment. They would try again in the morning.

When they reached the hotel Nan and Flossie saw Bert and Freddie talking to Mr. Ayler in a corner of the lobby. "Any luck?" Bert asked as the girls walked over to him.

Nan shook her head sadly and told him about the empty house.

"That's too bad," said Bert sympathetically.

"Well, you've certainly had luck in my case," Mr. Ayler said heartily. "Bert told me about Flossie's finding my attaché case and that the police know the name of the man who took it."

"And we'll find your plans, too!" Freddie declared.

"Speaking of plans," Mr. Ayler said, "I've had some strange news from my factory. It seems that one of the draftsmen, John Betz, has disappeared!"

"That's the man who dropped the papers when I bumped into him," Freddie remarked excitedly.

"Haven't they any idea why he's gone?" Nan asked.

"No, but my foreman is checking and will let me know as soon as he has any news."

The children said good-by to Mr. Ayler, promising to keep in touch with him. They joined the Lakeport school party for supper. Charlie and Nellie were waiting eagerly to hear the latest developments in the two mysteries.

"That empty house sounds spooky!" Nellie said with a shiver when Nan described their trip to Georgetown.

"We're going back again," Flossie declared. "We're not scared!"

"I hope the police find that man Kraus," Charlie said as he left Bert for the night.

The next morning after breakfast Nan tried to telephone the Georgetown house. An operator came on the line to tell her phone service had been discontinued. With a sigh Nan hung up and hurried to join the others for the morning's sightseeing.

The first stop was at the Capitol. "It's big, isn't it?" Flossie remarked as she got out of the bus. At once the small twin ran toward the long flight of steps which led up to the main entrance of the stately white building topped by its large round dome.

A guide met the group to take them through the building. He explained that the Capitol was the seat of government of the United States. "The Senate meets in one wing and the House of Representatives in the other," he said.

Next he pointed out the painting which circled the inside of the dome. "It shows important events in United States history." Then he led the way into a large circular room.

"This is called Statuary Hall," he remarked. "Among those statues around the edge of the room is one of a famous man from each state of the Union. Perhaps you'd like to examine them more closely."

The school children began to stroll about the room looking at the statues. At one point Bert and Nan stood together. Suddenly they stared at each other in surprise. They could plainly hear a conversation although there was no one near them!

"Meet me tonight at the Shishkabob Restaurant," a man's voice was saying. "We'll make our plans to escape."

"I'll be there," his friend replied.

At that moment the guide came up to the children. "See that mark on the floor?" he asked, pointing to a small black circle in the marble at their feet. "For some strange reason, a whispered conversation on the other side of the room can be clearly heard at this spot."

Quickly Nan looked around the large hall. Tourists walked about examining the statues. On the far side of the room two men stood deep in conversation. Both were of medium height. One was blond, the other wore a black beard!

"Look, Bert!" Nan whispered. "Those men over there! I think it was their voices we heard!"

Bert glanced over. "That bearded one looks

like the man I saw in the Ronda!" he said excitedly.

"I'm going to snap their picture before they get away!" Nan declared. She walked across the hall, pretending to be looking at the statues as she went.

When she reached the area where the men were standing, still talking busily, she stopped. Carefully she raised her little flash camera as if focusing on the statue behind the two men and pressed the trigger.

There was a sudden bright light as the flash went off. The men looked up, startled, and the next second they hurried from the room.

"I got them!" Nan cried happily, running back to Bert. "I'll have the film developed right away and show the picture to Mr. Ayler. Maybe he'll be able to recognize the men!"

"Good idea, Sis!" her brother agreed. "Did you see a scar on the bearded man's hand?"

"I was so excited trying to take the picture," Nan confessed, "that I forgot to look!"

Just then the guide clapped his hands from the center of the room. "If you will follow me, please, we will now go up to the gallery to see the House of Representatives in session," he called.

The school group gathered behind him and were led up an imposing stairway and into a long corridor. There were windows along one

Nan focused her little flash camera.

side and doors on the other. A uniformed guard stood before one of the doors.

"Please leave all cameras on the table," he directed.

Obediently the children took the cameras from around their necks and from their pockets. They placed them on the table near the entrance to the gallery.

The guard ushered the Lakeport visitors down the steep steps inside and showed them where to sit. They filed in. The four Bobbseys found themselves in the front row. They leaned forward and looked down into the House chamber.

There were rows of desks arranged in a semicircle around a raised platform. On this platform was another desk. Mr. Tetlow whispered, "That belongs to the man who presides over the meetings—the Speaker of the House."

At the moment one of the Representatives was making a speech. The school children were all quiet, listening to him. But suddenly angry voices could be heard. Danny Rugg and Jack Westley were arguing.

"Quit shoving!" Danny said loudly.

"I'm not shoving!" Jack protested.

The guard walked down the steps toward the boys. "Come on," he said sternly, motioning them to leave.

Mr. Tetlow stood up and gave the signal for

the others to follow. As Nan started to climb the stairs she noticed a man standing in the doorway. When he saw her, he disappeared.

"He's the one who was talking to the black-bearded man!" she thought. "I wonder what he was doing here?"

A few minutes later when she reached the corridor she saw the man again. He was just picking up her camera from the table!

"That's mine!" Nan cried out, hurrying toward him.

The man darted an angry glance at her and walked quickly down the corridor.

"Bert!" Nan said. "That man took my camera!"

"Stop!" Bert called. But the man paid no attention.

"Come on! Let's catch him!" the boy cried.

While the other children watched in surprise Bert and Nan raced down the corridor. When they got to the top of the stairs the man had just reached the bottom. He turned to the left and hurried away.

The twins ran down the stairs and followed the thief along the hall. It was crowded with people and Bert and Nan had to dodge in and out among them to keep the man in sight.

He stopped once and looked back. When he saw the children he started off again faster than before.

"He's turned a corner!" Bert exclaimed, beginning to run.

Passersby stopped and looked curiously at the two children dashing through the corridor. Bert and Nan followed the man to the rotunda. There he slipped easily through the crowd. The twins were delayed by a large group of sightseers who stood in the center of the hall gazing up at the dome.

When they finally got through, Nan was ahead. She reached the hall just in time to see the fugitive duck into an elevator.

"Stop!" she called to the operator. But the door closed and the car moved downward.

"Hurry, Bert!" Nan cried. She stepped into the other elevator as soon as the door opened. Her brother followed.

"Did he go down?" Bert asked when he had recovered his breath.

Nan nodded and turned to the elevator operator.

"What's down below here?" she asked.

"Offices and the subway," was the reply.

"The subway!" Nan repeated in surprise.

"Sure!" The operator grinned. "We have the nicest little subway in the world. It goes from here over to the Senate Office Building. Just turn left when you get off the elevator."

He opened the door and the children hurried out. They turned. In front of them was an incline leading down to two sets of tracks running off into a brillantly lighted tunnel.

A roofless metal car stood at the end of the right hand track. A little bell sounded, and the car began to move.

Nan clutched Bert's arm. "Oh!" she cried. "The thief's in that car!"

CHAPTER VIII

SHISHKABOB

"WE'LL follow him!" Bert declared, running down to the track.

"It's no use," Nan said sadly. "By the time the next car comes and we get over to the Senate Building, he'll be gone!"

"I guess you're right," Bert admitted. "We may as well go back."

When the two reached the rotunda again the school group was waiting. "Did you catch the man?" Freddie and Flossie called.

"No, he got away," Nan told them. "And so did the picture I took to show the police!"

As the children started out of the building, Flossie slipped her hand into Nan's. "You can have my camera, Nan," she said. "I don't use it much."

"Thanks, honey," Nan replied. Mr. Bobbsey had given his younger daughter a little camera for the trip, and Nan knew Flossie was very

71

proud of it. "I'll borrow it if I want to take a special picture."

"Okay," Flossie agreed.

Mr. Tetlow announced that they were to go to the Library of Congress next. "It's just across the street," he said, pointing to a huge marble structure not far away, "so we'll walk. Follow me and be careful crossing the street."

"Ooh! Look at the horses!" Flossie cried when they reached the building.

"Where?" Freddie asked. "I don't see any!"

Flossie giggled. "There! In that fountain!" She pointed toward a semicircular fountain at the base of the steps leading up to the library. At each side was a charging horse, water pouring from its mouth.

The small twins ran to the pool surrounding the fountain. "See the turtles!" Flossie exclaimed. She leaned over to look more closely at the big bronze figures half in and half out of the water.

"I'm going to pat this one!" Flossie stretched out her hand as far as she could. She teetered on the stone edge of the pool. "Oh!" she cried.

Then Flossie felt a hand grasp her arm and pull her back to safety. "Thank you!" she said, looking up into Nellie's face. "You saved me!"

Nellie laughed. "I saved you from getting wet, that's all!"

When the children stepped into the entrance

hall of the library, they gasped. It was dazzling —with white marble stairs and pillars and brightly painted walls and ceiling.

"No visitors are allowed in the main reading room," Mr. Tetlow explained, "but we can see it from the gallery." He led the way up two flights of stairs, then through a wide doorway onto a balcony.

The children lined up at the railing and looked down into the reading room. It was round and the tables were placed in circles. A little light shone over each reading desk.

Nan drew a deep breath. "It smells just like our library in Lakeport," she observed.

Miss Vandermeer heard her and smiled. "That's the odor of leather bindings and printing ink," she said. "All libraries smell like this!"

Bert had been hanging over the railing watching the people who were reading at the tables. Now he gave a start. "Nan!" he whispered. "Look at that man at the table just below here. Isn't that our friend with the black beard?"

Nan exclaimed, "Yes, I'm sure of it!"

"I want to see him!" Flossie stood on tiptoes and peered over the balcony, her little black pocketbook dangling from her hand. In her excitement it slipped out of her fingers.

Plop! The bag landed on the bearded man's

table! Startled, he looked up at the balcony. When he saw the Bobbseys, a look of rage came over his face. He stood up and hurriedly left the room.

"I want my pocketbook!" Flossie wailed.

"I'll get it for you," Nan offered. "And maybe I can see that man again!"

She ran down to the main floor, but he was not in sight. At the rear of the entrance hall Nan found the door leading to the reading room and went in.

A woman sat at a desk just inside. "I'm sorry," she said. "No visitors are allowed in here."

"My sister dropped her pocketbook over the balcony railing," Nan explained. "I just want to get it for her."

"In that case, you may go in," the librarian agreed, "but please be very quiet."

Nan tiptoed into the room and over to the desk where the bearded man had been reading. As she leaned over to pick up Flossie's purse, she glanced at the large book spread out on the table. It was a book of maps labeled "Potomac River and Chesapeake Bay."

"I must remember that," thought Nan.

The Lakeport group was leaving the building as Nan came out of the reading room. She hurried to catch up with them and gave the purse to Flossie. Nan then told Bert about the maps the man had been looking at.

"Nan," Bert whispered, "look at that man!"

"Why would he be looking at maps?" she asked, puzzled.

"Well, I remember from my geography that Washington is on the Potomac River," Bert remarked, "and the Potomac flows into Chesapeake Bay."

"Then maybe he has a boat and just wants to see where he can go!" she concluded.

The bus picked up the group and drove them back to the hotel. As the twins walked into the lobby, Mr. Ayler came up to them.

"I've been looking for you," he said smilingly. "I'm free tonight. I'd like to take you four to dinner."

"Goody!" Flossie exclaimed. "I love to go to restaurants!"

"We've had some excitement this morning," Bert told the inventor and described the events in the Capitol and the Library of Congress.

"Well, well," Mr. Ayler remarked. "I imagine I know where you'd like to go to dinner tonight!"

Nan's dark eyes sparkled. "The Shishkabob! The black-bearded man and his friend are going to be there!"

"Wait here a minute," Mr. Ayler directed. He walked over to the desk and held a short conversation with the clerk. Then he came back to the children.

"The Shishkabob is a foreign restaurant in

Georgetown," he told them. "The clerk says it's all right, so we'll go there. I've rented a car. We'll meet here at six o'clock and drive to the restaurant."

That evening when they reached the Shishkabob Mr. Ayler and the twins found it to be dimly lighted. There were tables in the middle of the room and booths around the sides. The Bobbsey group was shown to a large booth.

"What would you like to eat?" their host asked the children.

"I'd like a peanut butter sandwich!" Freddie spoke up.

"How about something a little more exciting?" Mr. Ayler suggested. "Have you ever eaten flaming shishkabob? Look over there by the door to the kitchen and you'll see."

The twins turned around. "Whee!" cried Freddie. "I wish I had my fire engine!"

A waiter was carrying what looked like a sword. On it were pieces of meat. The whole thing was blazing! In a moment the waiter reached a table, showed the food to a couple seated there, then blew out the fire.

"That's an old, old custom in parts of Europe," said Mr. Ayler. "The meat is usually lamb and there are mushrooms between the pieces. Now, do you Bobbseys think you would like to try some shishkabob?"

"Oh, yes," Freddie said quickly. "And I'm

Daddy's little fireman, don't forget so I should be the one to put out the fire."

The twins could hardly wait for their orders to be filled. It took two waiters to carry in the flaming swords, so all the children had a chance to blow. Meanwhile the waiters reached over the tops of the hilts of the swords and covered the little tins of lighted alcohol that had made the blaze.

"Isn't this *fun?*" Nan said as some of the meat was taken from the sword and served to her.

Everyone became quiet as they started to eat the delicious food. Suddenly they became aware of men's voices in the next booth.

"The Big Boss had better take care of us," one man was saying angrily. "I'll tell him so when we meet him at the monument tonight!"

"Ssh!" another voice cautioned. The conversation then continued in lower tones which the children could not hear.

Mr. Ayler looked puzzled. "That voice!" he murmured. "I've heard it somewhere before!"

Some time later three men came out of the booth. Flossie and Nan, who sat facing them, looked up from their dessert. At that moment two waiters walked over to stand by the booth. The twins could see little of the men as they left the restaurant, but noted that they wore raincoats and had hats pulled low over their eyes.

"I'm sure two of those men were the ones

Bert and I heard talking in the Capitol!" Nan exclaimed. "Can't we follow them to the monument, Mr. Ayler?"

"But we don't even know which monument they meant!" the inventor protested.

"It might be one of the most famous," Bert declared. "Let's go to all three—the Washington, the Jefferson, and the Lincoln Memorials!"

"Please!" Freddie and Flossie begged.

Mr. Ayler caught their enthusiasm. "Okay!" he said. He signaled to the waiter and paid the check.

By the time he and the twins got outside it had begun to rain. The colorful street lights glistened on the wet pavements. Mr. Ayler drove first to the Washington Monument. The tall white shaft was illuminated. No one was near it. The same was true when they reached the Jefferson Memorial. It, too, was lighted but deserted.

"There's just the Lincoln Memorial left!" Nan sighed. "If those men aren't there, I guess we've lost them."

A few minutes later Mr. Ayler drove up in front of the Lincoln Memorial and stopped. As he did, a short, stocky man ran down the steps and jumped into a waiting taxi.

The twins looked up at the huge, thoughtful figure of Lincoln, which showed clearly in the spotlights playing on it. They stood quietly for several seconds, then Nan broke the silence. "Isn't it lovely?" she said softly. The others agreed.

"There's no one here either," Bert said in disappointment.

Freddie's bright eyes, however, had seen a movement among the columns surrounding the building. He began to run up the long flight of steps, the others following. When they reached the top, there was no sign of anyone.

Freddie put his finger to his lips. "They've gone around the side!" he whispered, and ran to the corner.

The next second the others heard a *thump*. Bert hurried after Freddie. He had slipped on the wet marble of the floor and was stretched flat on his back!

"I'm sure there's no one here," Mr. Ayler declared when he had made sure Freddie was unhurt. "Now perhaps you'd better return to the hotel."

The disappointed young detectives climbed into the car and the inventor headed back to the center of town. They had gone only a short distance when Bert glanced out the back window.

"A black Ronda is following us!" he announced excitedly.

CHAPTER IX

BLACK BEARD

"THEN Henry Kraus *was* at the Lincoln Memorial!" Nan exclaimed. "And he *is* the man we saw at the Capitol and at the restaurant!"

"Perhaps the man we saw leaving in the taxi was the one they were meeting!" Bert guessed.

"The Big Boss!" Mr. Ayler agreed.

The children looked back from time to time. The Ronda was still behind them. When Mr. Ayler stopped in front of the hotel the black car slowed for a second, then sped away.

"That's queer," Bert observed. "Why should that man be following us?"

None of them could think of a reason. When the children met for breakfast the next morning they discussed this mystery and also the one about the lost china.

"I wish we could go back to Miss Pompret's grandmother's house," Flossie said as she finished her cereal.

"Maybe if we ask Mr. Tetlow, he'd let us go there instead of sightseeing this morning," Nan proposed.

"Good idea," Bert remarked. "Freddie and I will go with you."

Miss Vandermeer was standing with Mr. Tetlow when Nan made her request. The teacher explained that she and the Bobbsey girls had been to the house on Monday.

"I'm sure Nan remembers how to get there and that they will be all right," she told the principal.

"Very well," Mr. Tetlow agreed. "When you've finished your business at the house, take a taxi to the Wax Museum. We'll meet you there later this morning."

Nan thanked him and ran to tell the other twins. Later, on their way out of the hotel, the desk clerk called to Nan.

"Someone left a package here for you last night," he said and handed her a brown paper parcel.

"Who would leave a package for me?" Nan asked, puzzled.

"What is it? Open it quick!" Flossie urged.

Nan tore off the wrapping and stared in amazement. "My camera!" she cried.

"Something fell out." Freddie stooped and picked up a slip of white paper from the floor.

Bert read it aloud: KEEP YOUR NOSE

OUT OF THINGS WHICH ARE NONE OF YOUR BUSINESS.

"How sassy!" exclaimed Flossie.

Nan had quickly looked at the camera. "The film has been removed!" she cried. "Those men didn't want me to have their pictures! That's the reason the blond one took the camera."

"Maybe they followed us last night so they'd know where we're staying," Freddie suggested excitedly.

Bert ruffled his brother's blond hair. "I think you have something there, pal!" he said with a grin.

Nan checked her camera at the desk, and the twins ran out to catch the bus. When they reached the right stop in Georgetown, Nan pulled the signal cord. Once more they walked the cobblestone block to the Pompret house.

"The door's open!" Flossie called out as they neared the old building. She ran up the steps and rang the bell. It echoed through the house, but no one came to answer.

"That's funny," said Bert. "Someone must be here if the door's open!"

Flossie rang again, but there was still no answer. "Let's go in and 'vestigate!" Freddie urged.

"Do you think we should?" Nan asked nervously.

"The door's open. We may as well," Bert

replied. He stepped through the opening, the others close behind him.

Directly in front of them the children saw a steep winding stairway leading to the second floor. To the left was a living room and back of that appeared to be a dining room. The covered chairs which Nan and Flossie had seen before were still in the front room. There were no rugs on the floor or curtains at the windows. A broom leaned against the wall.

"Someone's been cleaning," Nan observed. "Maybe she's upstairs and didn't hear the bell. Let's go find out."

The children climbed the stairs which led to a narrow hall. Two bedrooms and a bath opened off it. The stairs continued up to another story.

The twins walked through the empty rooms and back into the hall. Suddenly they halted. Someone was coming up the stairs! Who was it? They waited breathlessly.

A small, stooped white-haired woman stepped into the hall. She looked surprised to see the children.

"Who are you?" she asked in a high, quavery voice.

Quickly Nan introduced herself and her sister and brothers and explained that they were friends of Miss Pompret's. "We rang, but I guess you didn't hear us," she concluded.

"Who are you?" she asked.

"I was in the basement," the elderly woman said. "I'm Della. I was Mrs. Pompret's housekeeper for many years."

"Miss Pompret didn't get the cream pitcher and sugar bowl to her tea set," Flossie spoke up.

When Nan explained about the missing pieces of china, Della shook her head. "Mrs. Pompret told me to send her granddaughter only the good china," she said. "The creamer and sugar bowl were chipped so I threw them out!"

"Threw them out!" Nan echoed in distress. "Where?"

Della thought a minute. "I put them in a barrel with other things I was getting rid of," she said. "It's probably still out back."

"May we look?" Flossie asked eagerly.

The woman nodded, and the children dashed downstairs, through the kitchen and out the back door. The barrel was not there.

"It's gone!" Flossie cried. "The china is lost!"

"What are you looking for?" a voice asked from the next yard.

The twins looked up and saw a little girl swinging under a tree. Nan told her they were searching for a barrel which Della had put out.

"A man took it early yesterday morning," the child said. "He has a shop and he's going to sell the things in the barrel."

By this time Della had come out of the house.

When she heard the little girl's story she brightened. "That must have been Mr. Ankarian. I told him he could have anything I threw out."

"Where is his shop?" Bert asked. "We could go there and get the china."

"It's just in the next block," Della told him. "It's called *The Oaken Bucket.*"

"Come on, let's go!" Freddie urged.

The four children waved good-by to Della and ran off down the street.

"There it is!" Flossie cried a few minutes later. She pointed to an old wooden bucket hanging out over the sidewalk.

Bert pushed open the door of the shop. As he did, a thin, frail-looking man with a little gray mustache came from a back room. He made his way through the cluttered space.

"What can I do for you young people?" he asked pleasantly.

Nan explained their errand, and Mr. Ankarian began to push aside various articles which were piled on top of one another.

Freddie spied an old sword. "We had our dinner on things like that last night!" he said proudly.

"Ah! You were at the Shishkabob?" the man asked. "Come, I show you!"

With a mysterious look he led the twins into the back room of the shop and opened the outside door. "There is the Shishkabob!" he said with a wave of his hand toward the narrow alley.

Just opposite was the back door of the restaurant. At that moment a slim man in a bright blue suit hurried up the alley and went into the restaurant. The children were still looking up and down the narrow lane when the man came out again and hurried off. This time he wore a black beard!

"Ooh!" Flossie squealed. "Doesn't he look funny!"

The man heard her. He darted an angry glance at the children and ran off down the alley.

"That's Henry Kraus!" Bert exclaimed.

By the time the boy had recovered from his surprise enough to take off after the man it was too late. He had disappeared.

"I lost him," Bert said sadly when he returned to the shop.

"Well, at least we know now that Henry Kraus's beard is false!" Nan explained.

Mr. Ankarian looked bewildered, so Nan explained that they suspected the bearded man of being a thief. "May we call the police from here?" she asked.

The shop owner gave his consent, and Bert talked to Mr. Hogan. The detective congratulated the children on their alertness and promised to have his men watch the Shishkabob.

"You wish to see the things I picked up from the Pompret house?" Mr. Ankarian asked as Bert turned away from the phone.

"We're looking for a special cream pitcher and sugar bowl," Nan told him. "Della says they were in the barrel in back of the house."

"Ah, yes, the one I picked up yesterday," the man remarked. "Now, let's see, what did I do with those things?" He looked around the cluttered shop. There seemed to be everything but a cream pitcher and sugar bowl.

"Could that be the cream pitcher?" Bert asked, pointing to a high shelf.

Nan and Flossie ran over under the shelf and peered up. There were boxes of different shapes and sizes, candlesticks, and even some old cowbells. Near the edge was a little white china pitcher with pink roses on it.

"That's it, Nan!" Flossie cried. "I'm sure it is!"

"May we see the pitcher?" Nan asked the shop owner.

"I'll get the ladder," he said and hurried into the back room.

"Let's see if we can find the sugar bowl too," Bert suggested.

The children walked about the room searching in baskets and on tables but without success.

"Look at the kitty!" Flossie cried. She ran

toward a big gray cat which had just come into the shop through the open door.

The cat gave Flossie a startled look and jumped up onto a high chest. From there it leaped to the shelf and stalked along it.

"Oh, she'll break the pitcher!" Flossie exclaimed.

The four children watched breathlessly as the cat moved along the shelf. It stepped carefully past the cream pitcher and they heaved sighs of relief. But the next second the cat's long tail swished against the china.

The flowered pitcher fell to the floor with a *crash!*

CHAPTER X

A DUMMY'S WARNING

"WOW!" Freddie exclaimed. "There's not much left of that cream pitcher!"

Sadly the Bobbsey twins surveyed the broken remains of the china. Tears gathered in Flossie's eyes. "Now Miss Pompret won't ever have it!" she said.

"Maybe we can mend it," Bert spoke up hopefully. "If it was already chipped, she shouldn't mind a few more cracks!"

"We can try," said Nan, looking a little happier. She told Mr. Ankarian the name of their hotel and promised to let him know if the pitcher could be fixed.

"I'll get you something to put the pieces in," the man said. He went to the back room again and returned with a small paper bag. Bert, Freddie, and Flossie knelt down, picked up the bits of china, and dropped them into the bag.

After another unsuccessful search for the

sugar bowl, Mr. Ankarian called a taxi for the children, and they were soon on their way to the Wax Museum. When they arrived the school group was already there. Mr. Tetlow paid the admission fee and handed a ticket to each pupil.

A young woman in uniform stood at the entrance to the exhibit rooms. She had a box in her hand. A voice said, "Please give me your ticket."

"Here's mine," Freddie said, holding it out toward the figure.

Danny, who was behind the little boy, gave a hoot. "You're dopey!" he jeered. "Can't you see she's a dummy!"

Embarrassed, Freddie dropped his ticket into the box and hurried on. The exhibition rooms were dimly lighted. But along the sides under bright spotlights were tableaux showing scenes from the history of the United States. The wax figures in them were very lifelike.

The children walked slowly past the displays. Among the first was one called "Columbus Discovering America." There was a wooden rowboat with three costumed figures in it. In the foreground were several palm trees and a sandy beach. Columbus was placed in the front of the boat as if about to step onto the land.

Nan and Nellie stopped to look at the group more closely. At that moment Danny and Jack came up. "Hey!" said Danny, "I think I'll get

in that boat and ride with Columbus!" He
began to climb over the low fence which
guarded the exhibit.

"You'd better not, Danny Rugg!" Nellie cautioned. "You'll get into trouble!"

"Go on!" said Danny. "Don't try to boss me!"

Before the girls could stop him, the bully
climbed into the boat. "Look at me!" he shouted.
"I'm discovering America!"

Danny began to rock the boat from side to
side. The figures in it teetered dangerously.

"Be careful, Danny!" Nan cried.

But the boy paid no attention. Suddenly the
figure of Columbus crashed over the side of
the boat!

At the noise, an attendant came running.
"What's going on here?" he asked sternly. When
he saw Danny in the boat and Columbus on the
floor, he became angry. "Get out of there at
once!" he ordered.

He picked up the wax figure and examined it.
Fortunately the soft sand around the boat had
broken the fall. The wig and cap had come off,
but otherwise there seemed to be no damage.

While the guard was picking up the figure,
Danny and Jack had run off. Nan and Nellie
walked on.

In the meantime Freddie had been standing in
front of a tableau marked, "Pocahontas Saves
Captain John Smith." It showed an Indian

chief seated on a tree stump. In front of him the figure of a man in old-fashioned clothes was stretched out on the ground, his hands tied behind him. Kneeling by his side was an Indian girl, while another Indian raised a club over the man's head.

"That looks exciting," Freddie said to himself. Then he gazed more closely. The man on the ground appeared to be breathing! But by the light of the overhead spot, Freddie could see that the figure was only wax.

"I guess they've got something inside his jacket to make it go up and down," the little boy decided. Then, as he continued to watch the "breathing" a voice came from behind him.

"That will happen to you if you don't cut out your snooping!" it said.

Freddie whirled around but saw no one. Then he caught sight of a guard standing in the corner. He walked over. "Did you speak to me?" he asked.

There was no reply. Freddie repeated his question and took the guard's hand. Quickly he dropped it. The man was a wax dummy!

Freddie shivered. "This place is spooky!" he thought.

Nan and Nellie walked up, and he joined them. He told Nan what had happened. "I wonder if it could have been Henry Kraus?" she said in a worried tone. "He might have fol-

The man was a wax dummy!

lowed us here from *The Oaken Bucket*."

They looked carefully at the other visitors they passed, but saw no one resembling the bearded man.

Soon Freddie became so interested in the tableaux that he forgot his fright. There was a lovely scene of Betsy Ross sewing the first American flag and another showing a ship sinking in the ocean.

"They sure look real!" Freddie commented.

"Yes," said Nan with a shiver. "They're creepy!"

By this time the children had reached the exit where the others were waiting. Freddie told Bert and Flossie about the strange voice which had spoken to him.

"I think you were just hearing things in that spooky place," Bert said teasingly. But Freddie insisted that someone had really warned him.

After lunch at the hotel, Nan bought a bottle of glue at the newsstand. "Come up to my room," she told the others. "Let's see if we can fix the cream pitcher."

Bert brought the bag of china pieces and carefully spread them out on the floor.

"This is like working a puzzle!" Flossie said as she picked up the biggest piece.

Freddie and Flossie carefully sorted out the bits that seemed to match. Bert and Nan glued them together. Finally Nan held up the mended pitcher. It was full of knicks and the glue had run in several places.

"Do you think it's really Miss Pompret's pitcher?" Flossie asked doubtfully.

"There's one way we can tell!" Nan reminded her. "Remember, Miss Pompret said each piece had a special mark on the bottom."

"Yes!" Flossie cried, "A lion in a circle!"

Carefully Nan turned the cream pitcher over to examine it. The others waited breathlessly.

"There isn't any kind of mark!" Nan said.

Bert took the pitcher. "You're right," he agreed. "But Mr. Ankarian *must* have the one that belongs to Miss Pompret. He took the barrel, and Della said she put it in there!"

"Let's go back to the shop and look around some more," Flossie suggested.

"Yes, let's!" Nan agreed. "I'll call Miss Vandermeer's room and ask her if it will be all right for us to go."

The teacher was sympathetic and suggested that the twins drive to the shop in a taxi. "We won't leave for our afternoon sightseeing until three o'clock. You should be back by then." Nan promised not to linger at the shop.

The four children hurried out to the street. A cab came along almost immediately, and they piled in.

The taxi was much faster than the bus and it seemed no time at all until it pulled up in front of *The Oaken Bucket*. Bert paid the driver while Freddie and Flossie dashed to the door of the shop and went in.

"Oh!" Flossie exclaimed. "Look!"

Bert and Nan joined the small twins. They gasped at the sight which met their eyes. Articles had been pulled from all the shelves and thrown on the floor. Chairs were toppled over. The place looked as if it had been struck by a great windstorm!

"What happened?" Nan finally said. "Where is Mr. Ankarian?"

"P'raps he ran away," Flossie suggested.

"Let's look around," Bert proposed. "Maybe we can find out who did this." He began to step over the objects which littered the floor.

The others followed as he picked his way through the debris. After a minute Freddie stopped. "I hear something," he said.

They all listened. There came the sound of a groan from the back room. Bert dashed ahead.

"Here he is!" he cried a second later.

By the time the others reached him Bert was helping Mr. Ankarian to his feet. "He was stretched out here on the floor!" the boy told his family.

"Can you tell us what happened?" Nan asked kindly.

Mr. Ankarian ran his hand over his face in a dazed manner. Then he said that two masked men had come into the shop when he was eating his lunch. One of them had knocked him down, saying, "This will teach you to mind your own business!" He remembered nothing after that.

While telling his story, Mr. Ankarian had walked into the front part of his shop. "Oh!" he cried when he saw the littered place, "they've ruined it!"

"We'll straighten it up for you," Nan said. "You sit down and rest."

"I do feel a little weak," Mr. Ankarian confessed, sinking into an old chair.

"One of these masked men might have been Henry Kraus," Bert guessed.

"But what were they looking for?" Nan asked, puzzled.

Bert brought in the ladder and climbed up to put articles back on the shelves as Nan handed them to him. Freddie and Flossie set the chairs upright again.

"That's fine," Mr. Ankarian said after a while. "You've got it back in shape again!"

"I'll just sweep the floor," Bert volunteered. "Then we'll be finished."

He got a broom and cleaned the floor. As he started toward the back room to replace the broom, he stooped and picked up a heavy piece of letter paper. Part of the top had been torn off, but a portion of an engraved address remained.

In the middle of the sheet were the letters H.T. and L.T. and 12:30 P.M. and 6:42 P.M. printed in black pencil. Bert wondered if he had found a clue.

"What does this mean, Mr. Ankarian?" he asked eagerly.

CHAPTER XI

AN UNFRIENDLY LOBSTER

MR. ANKARIAN took the paper from Bert and examined it. "I never saw this before," he said. "One of those masked men must have dropped it."

He gave the paper to Nan, who looked at it, puzzled. "What do you suppose it all means?" she said.

"I'm sure the part of an address at the top is Massachusetts Avenue," Mr. Ankarian remarked. "See, there is M-A-S-S."

"What is Massachusetts Avenue?" Freddie wanted to know.

"It's one of the main streets in the city," the man replied. "There are many embassies of foreign countries along it as well as homes of wealthy people."

Bert was still looking at the paper. "The only things I can think of for L.T. and H.T. are low tide and high tide. Could that be right?" he asked finally.

"Could be," Nan agreed thoughtfully, "and maybe the times of day written there are when the tide is either high or low."

"But why would anyone write them down?" Flossie asked.

"I don't know," Nan admitted. "It does seem odd."

"One of my good friends owns a fishing boat," Mr. Ankarian added. "He goes up and down the Potomac a lot. Maybe he could tell you what the marks on the paper mean and if those letters really stand for low and high tides."

"Oh, will you ask him?" Nan suggested eagerly.

"Of course. I'll call him right now." The shop owner went to the telephone and dialed the man's number. There was no answer.

"He may be out in his boat now," Mr. Ankarian said. "I'll try him again tonight and let you know what he says."

"That'll be great," said Bert. "We may have found an important clue!"

Nan was suddenly reminded of why the twins had come to the shop. She explained to the owner that they had mended the broken pitcher, but it was not the one that matched Mrs. Pompret's china.

"Della was sure she had put both the creamer and the sugar bowl in that barrel you took," Nan went on. "They *must* be here somewhere."

Mr. Ankarian scratched his head and gazed about the cluttered room. "You say they were cream colored with pink roses?" he asked. When Nan nodded he went on, "It seems to me I did see some china like that, but I can't remember what I did with it."

Nan explained that they must get back to the hotel, but asked Mr. Ankarian to let them know if he remembered anything about the Pompret china.

"I will think," he said slowly. "I will think."

When the taxi stopped in front of the hotel a short time later, the school bus was waiting. "Hurry!" Nellie called when she saw the twins leave the cab. "We're going down to see the docks and have supper there." As Nan walked down the aisle of the bus toward her, Nellie asked, "Did you find the china?"

"No, worse luck," Nan said and told her friend about their disappointment. "But we found a mysterious note which might have been dropped by the man who stole Mr. Ayler's space plans!"

Charlie moved up to sit near Bert and hear the news. By the time it was told, the bus had reached the river docks.

"Look, Bert!" Charlie poked his chum. "Isn't that a Ronda parked across the street?"

"It sure is!" Bert jumped from the bus as soon as it came to a halt. He dashed across the street to look at the car which was empty.

"It's the same license number," Bert said to himself. "Henry Kraus must be around here some place!"

Bert noticed a boy about eight years old seated on the curb. "Did you see a man get out of this car?" he asked him.

The boy nodded.

"Where did he go?"

The boy pointed toward a building nearby. It appeared to be a fish market.

"Thanks." Bert ran along the sidewalk and into the building. Inside was a narrow room with bins of fish down both sides. The floor was covered with sawdust.

Bert looked around. The room was deserted.

"What's the matter with the boy detective?" a sneering voice came from behind him. "Aren't you having any luck?" Bert whirled to see Danny Rugg coming in the door.

"I was looking for someone, but he isn't here," Bert admitted.

"Nice lot of fish though," Danny snickered. "Are you looking for a devilfish?" Danny walked along the bins pushing the fish around with one hand.

"You'd better stop that," Bert said. *"You* might find a devilfish."

"I'm not afraid of anything!" Danny boasted.

"Even lobsters." He ran over to a tank of water filled with lobsters and crabs.

"It'll serve you right if you get bitten," Bert warned.

"They won't hurt me!" Danny retorted. "I know how to pick them up." He dipped his hand in the tank and tried to pick up a big brownish-green lobster.

The bug-eyed shellfish suddenly opened one of its big front claws and fastened it on Danny's finger!

"Ow!" the bully yelled, jumping back. The lobster was still clinging to his hand. "Ow! Ow! Ow!"

Danny's cries brought a man running in from another room. He took in the situation at a glance. Directing Danny to stand still, he pried the claw open and freed the boy's finger.

"Your old lobster has broken my finger!" Danny raved. "It's all Bert Bobbsey's fault! He told me to pick it up!"

"I did not!" Bert replied angrily.

"Okay, boys," the man broke in. "Stop your arguing! I'll get something for this finger." He left and soon came back with antiseptic and a bandage which he put on Danny's wound.

Bert stayed behind when Danny hurried off. He asked if a bearded man had been in the market.

"Ow!" Danny yelled.

"Yes," the fish seller replied. "A man with a black beard was here a short while ago, but he ran to the street without buying any fish."

Disappointed, Bert joined the other children. They were walking along the shore looking at the line of fishing boats tied up there.

Charlie hurried to Bert's side. "Any luck?" he asked.

"No, Charlie. That man Kraus was in there but left."

"Mr. Tetlow says we're going to drive across the river to the Tomb of the Unknown Soldier, then come back here for a fish supper," Charlie reported. "We'll be on the docks a few minutes longer, though. I'll help you ask at some of these places about the man you're looking for."

Nan and Nellie joined the boys and also offered to inquire. The four children spread out along the waterfront to ask at the various boats and fish stands.

The first few people said they had not noticed a black-bearded man. But finally Bert stopped at a fishing boat named the *Susie-Q*. The skipper was working on the deck.

In answer to the boy's question, the man walked over to the rail. "Yes," he said, "a man with a black beard was here a little while ago. Queer actin' duck!"

"What did he want?" Bert asked eagerly.

"He was askin' if I ever took any passengers

aboard the *Susie-Q,*" the fisherman replied. "Do you?"

The man pushed back his cap and grinned. "I told him the only passengers I ever carried were fish!"

"Do you know where the man went?" Bert asked hopefully.

"No, can't say I do. The last time I saw him he was headin' back toward the Mall."

Bert remembered that the Mall was a wide green park which stretched from the Capitol to the tall Washington Monument. "Why would Kraus leave his car down here?" Bert wondered as he went toward the bus.

Nan, Nellie, and Charlie soon joined him. They had not been able to find out one single thing about the bearded man.

"I'd like to call Mr. Hogan and tell him about the car," Bert said to Nan. He received permission from Mr. Tetlow and ran into a nearby building.

"Thanks for the tip, Bert," Mr. Hogan said when he heard the story. "I'll send somebody down there to watch that car. If Kraus comes back, we'll pick him up. He doesn't live at the address he gave for his automobile license."

When all the children were in the school bus once more, they were driven across the river past the huge Pentagon Building.

"This is the headquarters for the Department

of Defense," Mr. Tetlow announced. "It is the largest office building in the world!"

"Boy, is it *big!*" cried Freddie.

Leaving the five-sided structure behind, the bus made its way into Arlington National Cemetery and up a hill to the tomb of the Unknown Soldier. The boys and girls got out and climbed the steps of the amphitheater. From this point they watched the impressive changing of the guard in front of the simple marble tomb. Freddie was wide-eyed as he observed the brightly uniformed sentry march back and forth, clicking his heels.

After a drive through the cemetery and a short visit to the southern-type mansion where General Robert E. Lee had lived, the bus returned to the waterfront. It stopped in front of a seafood restaurant.

"The Ronda is still parked down the road!" Bert told the other Bobbseys excitedly.

At Miss Vandermeer's suggestion all the children ordered fresh fish for their supper. As they were eating, Bert looked over toward Danny Rugg. He was struggling to get the meat out of a lobster claw. Bert called out:

"Hey, Danny, is that the claw I saw take a nip out of your finger?"

Danny glared, but said nothing.

Later when the bus arrived at the hotel, Bert and Freddie stopped at the newspaper counter to buy some post cards. Then they went to the desk to ask for their keys.

"Message for you," the clerk said, and handed Bert a folded slip of paper.

"Hey, Nan!" Bert called to his twin, who was on her way to the elevator. "I have a message to call Mr. Ankarian. Wait a minute, and I'll call him from the booth here."

Nan and Flossie ran back and stood beside their brother as he placed the call.

"This is Bert Bobbsey," he said when Mr. Ankarian answered the ring.

"Oh, yes, Bert. I called to tell you that I suddenly remembered what happened to that cream pitcher and sugar bowl!"

CHAPTER XII

BUCKET FIREMAN

"YOU remember what you did with the china?" Bert repeated. The other children gathered closer to the phone.

Bert listened for a while and wrote down a number. Then he thanked Mr. Ankarian and hung up.

"What did he say?" Flossie asked eagerly.

"Mr. Ankarian sold the china to a woman who came into his shop while he was unpacking the barrel," Bert replied. "Her name is Mrs. Wellington. Mr. Ankarian says she's nice but a little queer."

"Where does she live?" Nan asked.

"Let's go see her," Flossie added.

Bert explained that Mrs. Wellington lived in a large house on Massachusetts Avenue. "He gave me her telephone number. Do you want to call her, Nan?"

"Yes, please do, Nan," Flossie urged. "We have to get the tea set pieces for Miss Pompret!"

Nan dialed the number. When Mrs. Wellington came on the line, Nan introduced herself and explained that she and her sister and brothers were searching for some lost pieces of china.

"Mr. Ankarian, who owns the *Oaken Bucket* shop, thinks he may have sold them to you," she said. Nan listened for a few minutes, then replied, "Thank you. We'd like to come."

When she turned from the telephone, Bert asked eagerly, "What did she say?"

"Mrs. Wellington wants us to come to her house for tea late tomorrow afternoon," Nan told them. "She says we can see the china then and decide if it's what we're looking for."

"I'm sure Mr. Tetlow will let us go if we explain," Nan said hopefully.

Bert was silent a few moments, then said thoughtfully, "You know this is Wednesday and we're supposed to go home on the school bus Friday."

"Oh, no!" Flossie cried. "We can't go home yet!"

"That's what I think," Bert agreed. "We haven't solved either of the mysteries. If we could only stay a few more days!"

"Maybe if we called Mother and Daddy and told them, they'd let us stay!" Freddie spoke up.

"Yes, let's call them!" Flossie spoke up.

"We-ell," Nan said slowly, "we could try!"

Bert put in the call to Lakeport, and in a few minutes the twins were talking to their parents. When Mr. Bobbsey heard the children's plea to stay longer in Washington, he said, "Let us think about it. I'll call you early tomorrow morning."

"At least he didn't say no!" Nan remarked with a grin as they all went up in the elevator.

The next morning the twins gathered in Bert's room to await the call from their father. When it came they were excited.

"Your mother," Mr. Bobbsey said, "will take a plane for Washington to arrive this afternoon. You can all fly home on Sunday."

"That's neat, Dad! Thanks loads," Bert exclaimed. "We'll try our best to solve the mysteries real soon."

"Okay, son," his father replied. "I'll phone Mr. Tetlow and tell him our plans. See you Sunday!"

The twins hurried down to breakfast. When they finished eating Nan said to Bert, "I have to leave now. Nellie and I thought it would be fun to have a picnic on the way to Mount Vernon today. Miss Vandermeer is going with us to buy the food."

"Get something good!" Bert teased.

While he was waiting for the sightseeing trip to start, Bert telephoned the police to ask about the Ronda parked at the docks. The report was that no one had come back yet for the car.

"That's sure queer!" Bert thought as he went to join the other children.

Miss Vandermeer and the girls had returned. The picnic food was placed in the back of the bus, then the driver took off. The first stop was at the Archives Building.

"The most important permanent records of the Government are kept here," Mr. Tetlow explained as the group began to walk up the long flight of steps to the entrance. "The building is said to have the best burglar alarm system in the world."

"I guess we won't see Henry Kraus in here!" Bert said to Charlie with a grin.

The school children were led into the large, round exhibition hall. "In these cases in the center of the wall," Miss Vandermeer told them, "are the three most precious documents of the United States Government. I want you to look at the Declaration of Independence, the Constitution of the United States, and the Bill of Rights. You've read about them in school, and now here they are!"

The children peered into the cases and tried to read the faded, spidery writing. When each one had taken a turn they filed out and returned to the bus.

"We're going to stop at a picnic spot on the way to Mount Vernon," Mr. Tetlow an-

nounced. "Miss Vandermeer and the girls have
provided a picnic lunch for us."

There were shouts of delight from all the
boys except Danny. "Picnics are silly!" he muttered.

The bus sped along the beautiful Mount
Vernon Memorial Highway. It led to the home
of the first President of the United States.
Shortly before reaching Mount Vernon, their
driver pulled into a roadside park.

The children climbed out and set to work
cooking. In no time at all fires were burning in
three grills. Sticks and frankfurters were
passed.

"Everyone cooks his own hot dogs!" Nellie
called out.

"I'll cook yours!" Flossie volunteered to the
principal.

She put a wiener on the end of her stick and
held it over the fire. Soon the meat began to
sizzle.

At that moment Danny ran past. As he came
to Flossie he bumped into her just hard enough
to jostle her arm. The stick flew up in the air
and the frankfurter fell into the fire with a
hiss!

"Oh, Danny! You meanie!" Flossie sputtered. "You made me drop Mr. Tetlow's hot
dog!"

Quickly the principal grabbed the stick and

Flossie's frankfurter fell into the fire!

speared the frankfurter. He picked it from the fire and put the meat on a roll. "It's just the way I like it!" he told Flossie. "Well done!"

When the last bites of ice cream and cake had been finished, the bus continued on to the entrance of the Mount Vernon estate. The children got out and walked along a gravel path. In a short time they arrived at a long green lawn. A winding walk on each side led to a large two-and-one half-story white house.

"It's bee-oo-ti-ful!" Flossie cried out.

As the group drew nearer the house, Bert asked curiously, "What's it built of?"

"The outer walls are planks of wood cut to look like stone," Mr. Tetlow explained. "When the wood is freshly painted, sand is put on it. That gives the wood the appearance of stone."

The children followed the Tetlows and Miss Vandermeer into the house. They walked slowly through the rooms, which were elegantly furnished in the style of George Washington's time.

As Freddie was walking through a small second floor hall he noticed a line of buckets on the attic landing. They were high and narrow and looked as if they were made of leather.

"What funny fire buckets!" Freddie thought.

A few minutes later he glanced out the window of a room. A thin wisp of smoke caught his eye.

"Fire!" he cried.

Freddie dashed to the hall and grabbed one of the old fire buckets. He ran down the stairs and out onto the long porch.

"What are you doing with that bucket?" a guard called to him in a stern voice.

"I'm going to put out the fire!" Freddie replied, motioning toward the smoke. "Where can I find some water?"

The guard laughed. "The gardeners are just burning some trash outside the kitchen," he said. "Better give me the bucket. I'll take it back. But first I'll tell you about the buckets."

The man explained that they had been brought by George Washington to Mount Vernon from Philadelphia where he had lived while he was President. There was little fire-fighting equipment in those days, and each householder kept a supply of buckets on hand. They were made of leather and lined with tar.

"The leather buckets last longer than those of wood," he said.

"I wish I'd lived then," Freddie said wistfully. "Then I could have used them!"

Flossie and the older twins had followed Freddie downstairs and out of the house. They were relieved to see that there was no fire.

Nan suggested that the twins look at the kitchen. It was separated from the main house by a covered walk. A huge open fireplace took up almost an entire side of the room. In it iron cooking pots hung from cranes. On the walls were displayed various cooking utensils of the eighteenth century.

"Mrs. Washington sure used long-handled spoons," Freddie remarked.

Miss Vandermeer laughed. "Those are pewter ladles her cooks used to dish up soup and stews."

Nan was interested in the tin candle molds and the wooden flour scoops. Flossie pointed to a round, covered pan with a long wooden handle and asked what it was.

"A warmer," said the teacher. "Hot coals were put inside and the warmer was put into a bed or a carriage. They were even carried into church pews in bitter cold weather."

Bert and Freddie had wandered off down the lane.

"Hurry!" Freddie called. "I see a stable down there!"

On the way was a storehouse, a smokehouse where meats had been cured and smoked, and a washhouse with big wooden tubs. Here the family laundry had been done.

The last building on the lane was the old stable. By now all the twins were together and gazed at the stalls where Washington's horses had been kept. Old harnesses, saddles, and curry combs hung from nails on the wall.

"I thought we'd see some horses," said Freddie in disappointment. "Let's go!"

The twins walked back to the house and around to the front, which overlooked the Potomac.

"I guess we came in the back door." Nan giggled.

"I think that was a front door, too," Flossie declared. "This house doesn't have a back— just two fronts and two sides!"

Bert had been staring at a tall man who was walking across the lawn some distance from the house. He seemed to be heading toward the river.

"Say!" Bert exclaimed. "I think that's John Betz, Mr. Ayler's draftsman!"

"You mean the one who left the factory and never came back?" Nan asked in surprise.

"Yes. What's he doing here!" Bert cried out.

"I'll go over and tell him Mr. Ayler is in Washington if he's looking for him," Freddie volunteered. The little boy began to run across the lawn, with the other twins following.

Suddenly Bert cried out in amazement, "John Betz has disappeared!"

CHAPTER XIII

THE "HA HA" WALL

"WHERE did John Betz go?" Nan asked, puzzled. "There's nothing but lawn."

"Maybe he fell in a hole," said Freddie.

"Come on!" Bert urged. "Let's find out!"

He dashed across the lawn toward the river. The others followed. Suddenly Bert skidded to a stop.

"Hold it!" he yelled, stretching out his arm to stop Freddie, who was just behind him.

When Freddie and the girls came up to Bert they saw what had made him halt. The lawn suddenly dropped off steeply to a meadow several feet below.

"Oh!" Nan exclaimed. "There's a brick wall here. The top is level with this lawn and the bottom of it with that ground down there. Bert, it's lucky you saw it or we'd have had bad falls."

"Probably John Betz jumped down there when he vanished," Nan reasoned. "He's not even in sight now."

"And we don't know which way he went," Bert added, "so we'll have to give up our search."

As they were discussing Betz's disappearance Mr. Tetlow strolled toward the twins. "I see you've discovered Washington's 'ha-ha' wall," he remarked.

"I think it's a 'boo-hoo' wall!" Flossie said with an impish grin. "We almost fell over it!"

"Why was the wall built like this?" Bert asked curiously.

Mr. Tetlow said that in George Washington's time cattle, sheep, and horses were allowed to graze on the grounds. The first President had the wall built to keep the animals off the lawn in front of the house.

"They couldn't jump high enough to scale the wall," he explained, "and the wall wasn't visible from the house, so it didn't spoil the looks of the lawn."

After admiring the view up the Potomac River and looking through the attractive little museum, the school children boarded the bus for the ride back to Washington.

When Nan stopped at the hotel desk for her key, the clerk said, "Your mother has arrived. She's in room five-oh-two until tomorrow. When your friend Nellie Parks leaves, Mrs. Bobbsey can take her room next to yours."

"Oh, good," said Nan, and hurried off to tell

Bert and the younger twins the news. As the four started toward the elevator to see their mother, Mr. Ayler joined them.

"We saw John Betz!" Freddie announced excitedly.

"You did? Here in Washington?" The inventor looked surprised.

Bert described their glimpse of the draftsman at Mount Vernon. "We wanted to speak to him, but he got away before we could reach him," the boy explained.

A strange look came over Mr. Ayler's face. "Remember I thought I recognized the voice of one of those men at the Shishkabob Restaurant the other night?"

The children nodded eagerly.

"It has just come to me! The voice was John Betz's!"

"John Betz!" Nan exclaimed.

"He might be one of the thieves who stole your drawings!" Bert cried.

"That's something else to report to Mr. Hogan," Nan suggested. She told Mr. Ayler of seeing Henry Kraus's car parked by the docks the day before and the twins' unsuccessful search for him.

Mr. Ayler promised to call the detective and give him a full description of the draftsman.

The children hurried to their mother's room. When greetings were over, the twins told

Mrs. Bobbsey all that had happened in the four days they had been in Washington.

"Gracious! You certainly have had an exciting time!" she exclaimed. "I can see why you want to stay a little longer. I've rented a car to use until we leave, so perhaps I can help my young detectives!"

"Oh, Mommy, I'm so glad you're here!" Flossie threw her arms around her mother.

Nan reminded the others of the planned visit to Mrs. Wellington's that afternoon. "Could you take us there, Mother?" she asked.

Mrs. Bobbsey agreed to drive the children to the house on Massachusetts Avenue. "I have a school friend who lives in that neighborhood," she said. "I'll drop you off and call on her while you're at Mrs. Wellington's."

A short time later Mrs. Bobbsey drove up to a big house on Massachusetts Avenue and the twins got out. As she drove away Bert put his hand into his pocket. He drew out the piece of white notepaper he had found in the Georgetown shop.

He glanced at it, then up at Mrs. Wellington's house. "If this part of an address really means Massachusetts Avenue," he said, "it must be near here. The numbers are very close."

"Let's go look at the house," Freddie urged. "Maybe Mr. Kraus lives there."

Nan and Flossie were also eager to find the

address on the note, so the four children walked
up the street, peering at the numbers on the
houses.

"There it is!" Flossie suddenly called out.
She pointed to a large, imposing-looking house.
A semicircular driveway led to the front door.

"Look! The door's open!" Freddie cried.
"There's a man holding it."

"Goody!" Flossie said. "We can go in."

She started up the driveway.

"Flossie!" Nan called. "Come back!"

But at the moment a car drove up to the entrance and stopped. A man and two women got
out. One of the women paused to smile at
Flossie. "Are you coming in here?" she asked.

"Yes, please," the little girl replied. She
walked along beside the woman and into the
house.

"We must get Flossie!" Nan said desperately.
Followed by Bert and Freddie, she walked to
the door. The man inside bowed and held it for
the children to enter.

They walked into a crowded entrance hall.
Flossie was not in sight. The other three children were swept along with the crowd. Presently they found themselves in an enclosed
patio. In the center was a small pool with water
lilies floating in it.

This room, too, was full of people chatting
and laughing together. Some were East Indians.

"We must get Flossie," Nan said desperately.

The men wore turbans and the women flowing garments of bright colors. There were also tall Africans in long striped robes.

"We must get out of here," Nan cried. "I'm sure it's a private party."

"But where is Flossie?" Bert asked.

"I see her!" Freddie spoke up and started across the room to where Flossie stood, talking to the strange woman.

All at once Bert grabbed Nan's arm. "Look over there!" he whispered. "I'm sure that's Kraus in the pink turban!"

"Where?" Nan gazed around the room.

"Talking to that short, stocky, foreign-looking man! I'm going over and see if I can hear what they're saying."

"Oh, Bert, be careful! I think we ought to leave," Nan repeated nervously.

But Bert had begun to make his way around the patio to come up behind the two men. When he finally got near them they seemed to be having a discussion of some sort.

The short man was asking for something. Bert heard the man in the turban say, "You'll get them when I get paid, and not before!"

In reply the short man broke into a stream of words. The only one Bert could catch was "Saturday."

"I wish I could hear what he's talking about," Bert thought, "but he's so hard to understand!"

The boy edged nearer. The turbaned man raised his left hand and nervously rubbed the back of his neck. On his hand was a star-shaped scar!

"He's Kraus all right!" Bert told himself.

As the boy watched, the two men were joined by a tall stranger with white hair. They all shook hands and walked together into another room.

Across the patio Bert saw that Nan looked upset. "I guess we'd better get out of here," he decided. Bert glanced around. Flossie was with Nan, but Freddie was standing on the far side of the pool.

Finally Bert caught Freddie's eye and motioned him to go over to Nan. Freddie nodded and started forward. But just then an African guest wearing a high feather headdress came into the room.

Freddie was so busy looking at him that he forgot about the pool. The next moment there was a big *splash*. Freddie had fallen into the water!

CHAPTER XIV

A TREASURE HUNT

"GLUB, glub!" Freddie sputtered as he struggled to his feet. A water lily hung from one ear. A wave of laughter swept over the room.

Bert dashed up and helped Freddie step out of the pool. Several people rushed to ask if the little boy had been hurt.

Freddie shook his head. He was too embarrassed to speak. As Bert led his brother from the room he saw the bearded man come to the door with his stout companion. He nodded toward Bert and Freddie and said something to the other man.

When the boys reached the entrance hall, they found Nan and Flossie there. Nan was speaking to a plump, jolly-looking woman.

"I'm terribly sorry," he heard Nan say. "My little sister came in here by mistake. My brothers and I followed to get her. We didn't mean to break into your party."

The woman patted Nan on the shoulder. "Don't worry about it, my dear," she said. "As long as the little boy didn't hurt himself—he provided some unexpected entertainment for my guests! Perhaps we should let him dry off before you go."

"Oh, never mind. He'll be all right," Nan insisted. "It's warm outdoors."

When the four children reached the street Nan turned to Freddie. "You can dry out at Mrs. Wellington's."

When she rang the bell of the four-story house, Mrs. Wellington answered the door. She was a short woman with curly blond hair. She looked surprised to see Freddie with water dripping from his clothes. Quickly Nan introduced herself and the others and explained that her small brother had accidentally fallen into a pool.

"Come right in!" Mrs. Wellington urged. "Freddie can take off his clothes in a bedroom and I'll give him something to wear. I always keep a few things here for my grandchildren."

Mrs. Wellington's maid Mattie found a pair of shorts and a sweater for Freddie. Then she put his clothes in the automatic dryer. "They'll be ready in no time," Mattie assured him.

While Bert and Freddie were upstairs, Nan asked Mrs. Wellington if she might use her telephone.

"There's one in the library." She pointed to a room on one side of the narrow hall.

Nan called police headquarters and asked for Mr. Hogan. When the detective came on the line, Nan told him about seeing the bearded man in the pink turban. She gave him the address of the house where the party was being held.

Mr. Hogan left the phone but was back in a minute. "This case is really baffling," he said. "That house is the embassy of a foreign country. It's against the law for me to go in unless I'm invited, and I couldn't arrest anyone there."

"Can't you do anything?" Nan cried in disappointment.

"I can send a man up to arrest Kraus when he leaves the embassy," Mr. Hogan replied. "I'll get someone there right away!"

When the children joined Mrs. Wellington in the living room, she said, "We'll have something to eat and you must tell me about this china you're looking for."

Mattie brought in plates of little sandwiches, tiny cupcakes, and a pitcher of milk. It all tasted delicious. Between bites Nan and Flossie told their hostess about Miss Pompret and the family tea set.

"She says George Washington's granddaughter used it!" Flossie declared.

"My! How impressive!" Mrs. Wellington

exclaimed. "I do hope you can find it!"

Nan looked surprised. "But Mr. Ankarian says he sold the missing pieces to you," she reminded the woman.

"Really?" Mrs. Wellington smiled uncertainly.

Flossie threw Nan a bewildered glance. Hadn't Mrs. Wellington said yesterday that she had the cream pitcher and sugar bowl?

Mrs. Wellington stood up. "I must tell you something, children," she said. "I'm very forgetful. I may have bought the china from Mr. Ankarian. I buy a lot of things from him."

"If we could look at the pieces," Nan ventured, "we could tell if they were Miss Pompret's."

"Of course, you may see them," Mrs. Wellington said. "But the trouble is that I don't remember where I put them."

The woman appeared to be thinking, then her face brightened. "I know what we'll do," she remarked. "We can search for them!"

"You mean a treasure hunt?" Freddie asked.

"That will be fun!" Flossie exclaimed.

"But maybe Mattie knows where they are," Nan suggested.

Their hostess shook her head. "No," she said. "Mattie never pays any attention to things like that. You'll just have to look for them yourselves! You can start in the attic. I sometimes put things I buy up there. Search everywhere—closets, bureau drawers—any place!"

The children climbed the stairs to the fourth floor. Bert flipped an electric light switch as they reached the top step, but nothing happened.

"I guess it doesn't work," he remarked. The only light came from two small windows at the sides. The twins spread out over the large room and began to search for the china.

Suddenly Flossie gave a gasp. "Nan," she whispered, "there are some people standing over in that corner!"

Nan looked in the direction her sister was pointing. She could see several dim shapes—they were motionless!

"I'm sure they're not real people," Nan said and walked over to the corner. Then she began to laugh. "Look, Flossie," she cried, "they're dress forms!"

"Wh-what are dress forms?" Flossie quavered.

"Nellie's mother has some in her attic," Nan explained. "When ladies used to make their own dresses they fitted them on forms like these."

"They're spooky-looking just the same," Flossie declared.

The twins finally decided that the china pieces were not in the attic.

"Let's try the third floor," Bert proposed.

There were three bedrooms on this floor. The

twins looked in closets and pulled open drawers, but they did not find the missing china.

"We haven't looked in here!" Freddie called, putting his hand on the door of a closet in the third bedroom.

"Go ahead," Bert replied.

Freddie turned the knob, but the door stuck. He jerked the handle hard, and the door opened with a rush.

"Oh!" Freddie yelled. An assortment of odd-looking objects cascaded from the closet shelf and hit the little boy, almost burying him!

Bert rushed forward and helped Freddie to his feet. Then he picked up one of the fallen pieces. It was a black false face with a huge red mouth and staring eyes.

"Ugh!" Nan exclaimed. "That's horrible!"

"I think this is a collection of antique masks," Bert observed, picking up another. This one wore a wide grin, and its eyebrows went up to points in the middle.

"We'd better put them back," Nan remarked. Together she and Bert managed to stuff the queer objects onto the closet shelf.

The second floor also had three bedrooms, and the children set to work again. After a few minutes Nan called out, "I think I've found it!"

Bert and the small twins ran over to her. Nan pointed to a table. On it was a round hatbox. A paper label on the top read: *China*.

It was a black false face with a huge mouth and staring eyes.

"Goody!" Flossie cried. "Open it quick!"

Carefully Nan untied the box and raised the lid. The others watched breathlessly as she lifted the tissue paper. Underneath was an old-fashioned hat trimmed with ribbons and flowers!

"Oh, no!" Bert exclaimed in disappointment.

"Maybe if we find a box marked *Hat,* it will have the china in it!" Flossie suggested with a giggle.

The children took up their search once more. When they reached the kitchen Mattie assured them the cream pitcher and sugar bowl were not there. "Mrs. Wellington never puts things where you'd expect to find them!" she said with a chuckle.

After a thorough search of the dining room and library, Bert went into the entrance hall. Behind the winding stairway stood a small sofa.

"Hey!" Bert called when he saw a box on the sofa. "Come look at this!" He pointed to the label. On it were printed the words: *Cousin Susie's Hat.*"

Were the china pieces in the box? Bert quickly opened it.

CHAPTER XV

THE DESERTED HOUSE

THE twins leaned forward as Bert took the lid from the box. Flossie squealed, "There's the cream pitcher! I know it is!"

Bert carefully lifted the pitcher. Then under a layer of tissue paper he found the sugar bowl! "Well, what do you know!" he said, grinning proudly. Then he carefully carried the pieces into the living room and set them on a table.

"Oh, you have the china!" Mrs. Wellington said in a pleased tone. "I'm so glad."

"We think they're the ones," Nan remarked, "but we have to see if they have the right mark." She turned over the cream pitcher to look.

On the bottom was the tiny figure of a lion in a circle!

"Goody! We've found Miss Pompret's china!" Flossie danced around the room.

"I'm sure Miss Pompret will want to buy the creamer and sugar bowl from you," Nan said to Mrs. Wellington. "Will you sell them?"

"Certainly not!" Mrs. Wellington replied with a twinkle in her eye. Then, seeing Flossie's downcast look, she went on, "I shall be delighted to *give* them to Miss Pompret. After all, they belong to her."

Flossie ran over and threw her arms about Mrs. Wellington. "You're nice!" she said.

"Thank you so much," said Nan.

"And thanks for the good food," Freddie added. "I'd like my own clothes now, please."

"They're upstairs," said Mattie, who had come to the door.

Freddie ran up to change. In the meantime Mrs. Wellington packed the china pieces into the hatbox again and handed it to Nan. "Come see me again," she urged as she opened the door for them.

"We will!" they promised.

When they reached the street Mrs. Bobbsey had not yet arrived. It was just before the dinner hour, and Massachusetts Avenue was crowded with cars coming from both directions.

"Mother's probably caught in the traffic," Bert remarked. "Let's walk down to the embassy and see what's going on."

The twins strolled along the street until they reached the large house where they had gone earlier. This time it looked very quiet. The front door was closed.

Bert noticed a police car just pulling away

from the curb. He hurried forward and called out to the officers in it. They stopped.

"I'm Bert Bobbsey," the boy explained. "Mr. Hogan said he'd send someone up here. Did you find Mr. Henry Kraus?"

The policeman beside the driver replied, "No, we've been waiting here for an hour, and no one with a black beard and a turban has come out. The party seems to be over, so we're leaving. Better luck next time, boy!" He gave the signal, and the car drove off.

"Aren't we ever going to catch that man?" Freddie asked impatiently.

Bert looked discouraged. "He's a slippery person, all right!" he said sadly.

The twins turned back to Mrs. Wellington's house. They stood in front, still looking toward the embassy. As they watched, a car came up the driveway and stopped at the door of the big house.

"Here's Mommy," Flossie announced a second later, as an automobile drew up.

"Hop in," Mrs. Bobbsey called, leaning over and opening the door.

Nan had been watching the embassy door. Now she cried out, "There he is!"

A man had come out and jumped into the waiting car.

"But he didn't have a beard!" Flossie objected.

"No, but I'm sure he's our man!" Nan insisted. "Mother, please follow that car." The children scrambled in beside her.

Mrs. Bobbsey hesitated a moment, then pulled into the street and worked her way through the traffic until she was just behind the other car. It was painted in two tones of gray with a light top.

"Suppose you tell me what this is all about," Mrs. Bobbsey said as she followed the gray car.

Nan told about the twins' visit to the embassy. "And Henry Kraus was there!" Bert declared. "I'm sure he was the man in the pink turban!"

"And he's in that car we're following!" Nan added.

"If we find out where he's going, we can call Mr. Hogan and tell him," Bert explained.

"All right," Mrs. Bobbsey agreed. "I'll keep him in sight as long as I can."

On they went for block after block. The cars grew fewer as they reached the outskirts of the city. The gray car picked up speed.

"I don't like to drive so fast," Mrs. Bobbsey protested. "Perhaps we'd better not go any farther."

"Please, Mother!" Bert urged. "We don't want to lose Kraus again!"

By this time the driver of the other car seemed to realize he was being followed. He drove faster and faster. The Bobbsey car was being left behind.

Suddenly a road sign loomed up ahead of them. It read: "Construction ahead. Travel at your own risk." The gray car shot by the warning onto the rough road.

After a second's hesitation Mrs. Bobbsey followed. Their automobile bumped along, the twins hanging onto the sides to keep from being thrown against the roof.

"We're gaining on them!" Bert cried from his place on the front seat.

Suddenly the gray car hit a wooden "horse" at the side of the road. The rack swung around into the middle of the road.

"Look out!" Bert yelled.

Quickly Mrs. Bobbsey swerved the car. It skidded on two wheels and came to rest at the edge of the roadside ditch.

"You're great, Mother!" Bert said admiringly.

His mother smiled nervously. "Just the same I think this has gone far enough. We're out in the country and it's getting dark. We must go back!"

"Look!" Nan pointed ahead. "The gray car is turning down that road. Please follow it just a little longer, Mother!"

Mrs. Bobbsey started the engine again. "All

right," she agreed, "just a few more minutes."
She drove on until she came to the side road and

turned into it. The gray car was far in the
distance.

By this time it was dark and Mrs. Bobbsey

switched on the car lights. Suddenly Nan cried out, "Oh, the gray car's gone!"

"We've lost the bad man!" Flossie wailed.

"He drove around that house up there," Freddie declared.

In the glow from the car's headlights the Bobbseys could just make out an old, dilapidated-looking structure which stood across the road from a wooded section.

"Are you sure, Freddie?" Bert asked doubtfully. "It looks deserted."

"I saw him go in," Freddie insisted.

"I'm not going to drive in there," Mrs. Bobbsey said firmly. She stopped the car as if about to turn around.

"Wait, Mother!" Bert pleaded. "Let me out. I'll sneak around the house and see if the car's there."

"Why don't we all go?" Nan suggested. "Maybe there's a flash in the glove compartment of this car that we could use."

Quickly Bert pulled open the little door. A small flashlight was tucked among a few road maps.

"You're right, Sis," he said, picking up the flash. "Come on, let's go!"

They all got out of the car, and with Bert guiding their way with the light, the Bobbseys began to creep along a rutted lane toward the side of the old house.

"It's spooky!" Flossie said with a little shiver.

"I don't think anyone lives here!" Nan commented in a whisper. "Look at that house!"

The porch was sagging, and most of the windows were broken. Tall weeds smothered the rundown place.

Suddenly a gray shape dashed across the lane in front of them. Flossie screamed. "Wh-what's that?" she quavered.

"Aw, it's just a cat, silly!" Freddie told her disgustedly.

"Oh!" said Flossie in relief.

When the Bobbseys reached the back of the house, Bert shone the flashlight around. A few old farm implements were scattered about, but that was all. There was no gray car.

"You must have been dreaming when you saw it turn in here, Freddie!" Bert said teasingly.

"I saw it, I know I did," Freddie repeated.

"Let's get back to our car," Mrs. Bobbsey said nervously. "I don't like this place!"

Bert lighted the path again and they made their way to the road. As Mrs. Bobbsey slid behind the wheel, Bert cried out, "For Pete's sake!"

"What's the matter?" his mother asked, puzzled.

Bert was racing around the car. In a moment he cried out, "The tires! All of them are flat!"

CHAPTER XVI

ABOARD THE "FLYING S"

"FOUR flat tires!" Nan echoed her twin. "How could that have happened?"

"Someone let the air out!" Bert said grimly.

"But who?" Mrs. Bobbsey asked, getting out and glancing around nervously.

"Probably the man who was driving the gray car saw us stop. While we were behind the house, he came back and did this."

"What are we going to do now?" Flossie wailed.

Bert suggested that he walk back to the highway and try to flag down a car to bring them help.

"No, I won't let you go alone, Bert," his mother declared. "It's too dangerous. That horrible man might still be around!"

As the Bobbseys stood discussing what to do, they saw a small light appear in the distance. It came steadily toward them. They waited breathlessly.

"It's a boy on a bicycle!" Freddie cried at last.

As the figure drew closer Bert saw that Freddie was right. "Hello there!" Bert called.

The boy brought his bicycle to a halt and stepped off. "Hi!" he said. "You all in trouble? I'm Jimmy Preen."

"Is there a garage nearby?" Mrs. Bobbsey asked. "Our tires are flat."

Jimmy looked at the car in surprise. "No'm," he said, "there's no garage around here. But if you just need air in the tires, my daddy could fix 'em for you. He has a pump."

"Just what we want!" Bert exclaimed. "Could you get your father?"

"Sure!" the boy agreed. "I'll bring him right quick!" He mounted his bike and pedaled down the road. In a few minutes he was out of sight.

It was growing chilly so Mrs. Bobbsey and the twins got back in the car to keep warm. While they were waiting, the children told their mother about their search at Mrs. Wellington's for the china pieces.

"We found them!" Flossie said happily. "They were in a box marked 'Cousin Susie's hat.'"

Mrs. Bobbsey laughed. "That seems like a strange place to keep china," she remarked. "However, I think you were very clever to find it. I know Miss Pompret will be pleased."

Just then headlights appeared in the distance, and shortly after that a car stopped behind theirs. Jimmy and Mr. Preen, a tall, thin man stepped out.

"These are the folks I told you about," the boy said to his father as they both came over to the Bobbseys.

The man walked back to his car and pulled out a hand pump. "Jimmy tells me you need a little pumpin'," he drawled.

"We'd be very grateful if you could put enough air in the tires to get us to a service station," Mrs. Bobbsey said. "Some joker turned the valves."

Mr. Preen set to work with both his son and Bert helping. In a short while the tires were full of air again. Mrs. Bobbsey picked up her purse to pay the man.

He raised his hand. "You don't owe me anything, ma'am," he said. "I'm always glad to help out." Followed by his son, he got in his car, waved, and drove away.

"He was a nice man," Flossie said as she climbed into the back seat with Freddie. The others agreed.

Mrs. Bobbsey drove to the highway, then turned toward the city.

"I'm hungry," Freddie declared, so his mother stopped at a restaurant, and they had a late supper.

It was nine o'clock when the Bobbseys finally reached the hotel. The desk clerk handed Bert a message which asked the boy to telephone Mr. Ankarian. Freddie and Flossie were sleepy and went up to their rooms. But Nan and Mrs. Bobbsey waited for Bert to make the call.

"I finally reached my fisherman friend, Joel Stannard," Mr. Ankarian said. "He has invited you Bobbseys to go out on his boat tomorrow. You can show him that note then."

"Sounds great!" Bert cried. "Aren't you going?"

"I can't leave my store," the shopkeeper answered. He gave Bert directions for finding Captain Stannard's boat, which was called the *Flying S*.

Bert relayed the message to his mother and sister. "You'll go, won't you, Mother?" Nan asked.

"Why don't you invite Mr. Ayler to go with you?" Mrs. Bobbsey replied. "It's his mystery you're trying to solve. I can keep busy doing some shopping and sightseeing."

"Call him now, Bert," Nan suggested, "and see if he'd like to go."

The inventor accepted the invitation gladly and said he would drive the children to the dock.

The next morning the twins were up early. They had a farewell breakfast with the school party from Lakeport. When the bus was loaded and ready to leave, the four Bobbseys lined up to say good-by to Mr. and Mrs. Tetlow, Miss Vandermeer, and their young friends.

"I'm glad you found Miss Pompret's cream pitcher and sugar bowl," Nellie whispered to Nan.

"Good luck in solving Mr. Ayler's mystery," Charlie said as he swung up into the bus.

"I'll bet the F.B.I. is scared you'll put them out of business!" Danny taunted from his window seat.

All the children waved and called good-by as the bus started off down the street. Then Mr. Ayler drove up and the twins piled into his car. They had no trouble finding the *Flying S*.

As Mr. Ayler parked the car, a young man with twinkling blue eyes called from the deck of the fishing boat. "Right this way. Glad to have you aboard!" He helped the twins across the narrow plank which linked the boat to the dock. They introduced Mr. Ayler to the captain.

"I hear you children took care of my friend Ankarian when someone broke into his shop," he said when they were settled.

"That's when we found the odd note we want you to look at," Bert replied.

"Okay," the fisherman agreed. "But first we'll start down the river. I'll look at your

"Right this way," he said. "Glad to have you aboard."

paper when we anchor a little later to eat the picnic lunch I brought."

The breeze was fresh on the river, and the children enjoyed watching the sailboats as they whipped along.

"We don't get very large vessels this far up the river," Captain Stannard told them. "It's too shallow. But the Potomac flows into Chesapeake Bay, and there are many ships down there. I've seen freighters from all over the world anchored in the bay."

About an hour later the fisherman asked his passengers if they were hungry. "I am!" Freddie spoke up eagerly.

Mr. Ayler laughed. "I imagine we're all ready to eat," he said. "This river air gives one a good appetite."

"Would you like to help, Nan and Flossie?" the boatman asked when he had anchored the vessel. "I have a little stove in the galley. That's what a kitchen is called on a boat, you know."

The girls gladly agreed and soon were setting out paper plates and napkins marked the *Flying S,* while the captain fried fish and crisp potato slices.

"Mmm! This is yummy!" Flossie exclaimed a little later as she bit into a large fish sandwich.

After the last bit of fish had been eaten, their host produced oranges and cookies.

"I like galley food!" Freddie announced.

"So do I!" Flossie agreed.

When Bert finished his third cookie, he asked if he might take a few of the paper napkins as souvenirs.

"Help yourself," the genial captain said.

Bert took six of them, then he pulled the torn note from his pocket. "Do you think these letters stand for high tide and low tide?" he asked, passing the paper to the fisherman.

The captain studied the letters and figures. "H.T. and L.T.," he read aloud. "12:30 P.M. and 6:42 P.M. Hmm," the fisherman murmured. "I suppose they could stand for high tide and low tide. But I'm not sure just where the times would fit these tides."

Suddenly Bert had an idea. "I wonder—" he began thoughtfully.

"What?" Nan asked eagerly.

"Well—we know that John Betz is involved with Henry Kraus, and we think Kraus dropped this paper in Mr. Ankarian's shop."

"Who are John Betz and Henry Kraus?" Captain Stannard asked curiously.

Bert quickly told him about the mystery of Mr. Ayler's stolen plans and Betz's and Kraus's connection with it. "When we saw John Betz at Mount Vernon he was walking toward the river. So perhaps these notes have something to do with the Potomac!"

"You mean"— Nan was wide-eyed—" that these times and tides are at Mount Vernon?"

Captain Stannard had lifted anchor, and they were once more on their way down the river.

"Are we almost at Mount Vernon?" Bert asked.

The captain nodded and pointed ahead. In the distance the children could see the Washington home on the hill.

"It's almost twelve-thirty," Nan observed. "Can you tell if it will be high tide when we are opposite there?"

"I can tell you now that it won't be!" Captain Stannard replied.

"Oh!" Bert sounded disappointed.

The fisherman took a chart from the wall. "However," he went on when he had studied the figures for a few minutes, "it will be high tide along here at twelve-thirty tomorrow."

"Tomorrow is Saturday," Nan commented.

"Saturday!" Bert jumped to his feet. "That's it! When the fat man was talking to Kraus at the embassy, he mentioned Saturday!"

"Then something is supposed to happen on the river near Mount Vernon at twelve-thirty tomorrow!" Nan cried excitedly.

"Either on or near the river," Bert agreed. "Maybe Betz left some sort of signal when he was out here yesterday!"

"Let's watch along the shore," Freddie suggested.

Captain Stannard was becoming almost as interested as the children. "I'll run as close as I dare," he volunteered, "while you all keep a lookout."

He turned toward the shore and steered along it. The children scanned the ground as they moved slowly downstream, but looked up as the boat passed Mount Vernon.

The *Flying S* cruised in and out of several small coves. Then in a cove just south of Mount Vernon Freddie spotted a pole sticking out of the ground near the water line.

"Look!" he called. "There's something fastened to the top!"

CHAPTER XVII

YOUNG POLICE HELPERS

"LET'S go see what's on the pole!" Flossie urged.

Captain Stannard explained that he could not run the *Flying S* very near it, but someone could go ashore in the dinghy. It was decided that Bert and Mr. Ayler would investigate.

The small boat was lowered, and the inventor took the oars. He rowed close to the pole. Bert stood up and peered at the object fastened to it.

"It's a map of the Washington area!" he exclaimed in surprise. "I'll take it off so we can see it."

Mr. Ayler shook his head. "I don't think we'd better," he objected. "It's probably a signal of some kind, and the police should know about it."

"Let's tell Mr. Hogan," said Bert. "And about the tides, too."

"Right. I suggest we get back to Washington as soon as possible," Mr. Ayler suggested.

He turned the dinghy around, and they made their way back to the *Flying S*. The other children were puzzled when Bert told them of the map on the pole.

"We want to let the police know about it as soon as possible," he told the captain.

Nan had been wrinkling her forehead in deep thought. Finally she said, "It would be easier if the police could reach that cove from the land."

"You're right, Sis!" Bert cried. He turned to Captain Stannard. "Is there a road that runs along the river?"

"Sure!" the fisherman replied. "But I don't know just how far back from the water it is at this point."

"If some of us could find our way to the road from the cove," said Bert, "we could show the police how to get there!"

This idea was discussed by the twins and the two men. It was finally decided that Bert, Nan, and Mr. Ayler would go to shore and find their way through the woods to the highway. Freddie and Flossie would ride back to Washington on the *Flying S*.

"We'll all meet at Mr. Hogan's office," Bert said.

"Okay," the captain agreed. "I'll anchor and row the three of you to shore."

Freddie and Flossie hung over the rail and

watched as the little boat reached the edge of
the cove. Mr. Ayler and the older twins stepped
out and waved toward the *Flying S*. Then they
started off through the woods and Captain Stannard rowed back to the fishing boat. A few
minutes later it was headed up the Potomac toward Washington.

On shore the three explorers found that the
ground rose steeply from the water. It was
covered with undergrowth and trees. No road
was visible.

"We must be a long distance from the highway," Mr. Ayler remarked as he followed Bert
and Nan through the woods.

Suddenly Nan stopped. "We ought to mark
our path or we'll never be able to show the police how to get to the cove," she observed.

"We could blaze the trees," Mr. Ayler suggested, pulling out his penknife.

Bert had reached into his pockets. Now he
took out several white paper napkins he had
tucked in during the picnic. "How about using
these?" he suggested. "They'd be easier and
quicker to spot than tree blazes."

Nan added, "We can fasten bits of the paper
to branches of the bushes as we go along."

Mr. Ayler and Nan each took a napkin. As
they moved up the slope they tore off small
pieces and stuck them on the ends of the
branches.

Nan was in the lead. Suddenly she stopped and motioned for the others to do the same. Silently she pointed ahead to an indistinct shape against a tree trunk.

"A man?" Nan whispered.

The three crept forward cautiously. The figure did not move. All at once Bert began to laugh. "It's not a man!" he said. "It's a big bundle of some sort."

He and his twin ran to the tree. "It's a duffle bag!" Bert cried. "Someone must have left it here." He turned the heavy bag over. On one side stenciled in large white letters was the name: *J. Betz.*

"John Betz!" Nan exclaimed. "So he *did* come down this way!"

"He must have been looking for the cove yesterday when we saw him!" Bert said.

"But why would he leave his duffle bag down here in the woods?" Mr. Ayler asked.

"My guess is that he is planning to meet someone in the cove and make his getaway," Bert said. "He left the bag here and will pick it up tomorrow when he's ready to leave."

"Maybe we can catch him when he comes to get it," Nan suggested.

"We'll try," Bert agreed as they placed the duffle bag against the tree again and continued on their way.

A few minutes more brought them to the top

"It's a duffle bag!" Bert cried.

of the little hill. "There's the highway!" Nan called out.

"We're in luck!" Mr. Ayler remarked as they stepped out of the woods. "The bus to Washington must stop right here. See, there's the sign."

Bert went up to the signpost and looked at the schedule painted on it. "A bus is due in twenty minutes," he told the others.

Near the sign was a bench, so the three sat down to wait. When the bus came, it turned out to be a local one which stopped at each small settlement and shopping center. It was more than an hour before Mr. Ayler and the twins reached Washington.

They hailed a taxi and drove to Mr. Hogan's office. The detective was amazed at the story Bert and Nan told. "You children have done a good job!" he praised them. "We ought to catch all those crooks tomorrow."

Mr. Hogan explained that since the cove was in the state of Virginia, he would have to allow the Virginia police to handle the capture. "I'll get in touch with them right away," he promised. "You three will be able to show them how to reach the spot where the map is."

"Don't you think there ought to be someone out on the water to catch the thieves if they try to escape in a boat?" Bert suggested. "Captain Stannard could show the police the cove from the river."

"Good idea. I'm sure the Virginia police have a launch for that sort of thing," Mr. Hogan assured him.

While the detective was talking to the captain of the Virginia State Police, the door of his office opened. Freddie, Flossie, and Captain Stannard walked in. Bert quickly told them about finding the duffle bag.

"We have it all planned," Mr. Hogan said as he turned away from the telephone and greeted the newcomers. "The Virginia police will send a launch to the Washington dock tomorrow morning to pick up Captain Stannard. They'll also send a car to your hotel for Bert, Nan, and Mr. Ayler."

After thanking Captain Stannard for their exciting river trip, the twins drove back to the hotel with Mr. Ayler. Mrs. Bobbsey had returned from her shopping trip and listened to the account of the day's adventure.

"Tomorrow should be very exciting for you," she said. "I must represent Lakeport at a Red Cross meeting in the morning, but I'll hurry back to hear what happens. I'll take Freddie and Flossie to the dock first."

Early the next morning Bert received a call from Mr. Ayler. "I've just heard from my friends in the Pentagon," he said. "They want me for a conference this morning. I won't be able to go to Virginia with you."

"I'm sorry," Bert replied. "We'll call you as soon as we get back!"

A short time later, two Virginia state policemen arrived at the hotel. They introduced themselves as Officers Crane and Squier. "Are you sure you can point out this place?" one of them said to Bert when he learned that Mr. Ayler would not be able to go with them.

Bert and Nan assured the officers that they could locate the cove from the land, and Nan added, "We left a paper trail."

"And it goes down the hill from near a bus stop," Bert remarked.

"Okay," Officer Crane said. "Let's go!"

Mrs. Bobbsey had left earlier with Freddie and Flossie. When they reached the dock a trim police launch was waiting.

"Captain Stannard hasn't shown up," the skipper said to Mrs. Bobbsey. "My name is Webster. I'm afraid if we're to be down the river by noon we'll have to start soon."

"Where do you s'pose Captain Stannard is?" Freddie asked. "He said he'd be here!"

A man lounging on the dock walked up. "You waitin' for Stannard?" he asked Officer Webster.

"Yes. Do you know where he is?"

The man explained that Captain Stannard had taken a party of fishermen out early and had expected to be back. "I guess somethin's happened to keep him."

The police skipper looked uncertain. "We'll have to go without him, but how will we know the place on the river these crooks are supposed to be meeting?"

Freddie spoke up. "Flossie and I can show you. We know where the cove is!" Flossie bobbed her head vigorously.

Officer Webster looked questioningly at Mrs. Bobbsey. "I'm sure they can find it if they say they can," she said. "But are you sure you want to take them along?"

"Yes, of course. And we'll take good care of them. Well, let's shove off. I don't want to be late."

In the meantime Nan and Bert and the two police officers had reached the bus stop. The troopers parked their car, and the four stepped into the woods. Quickly Nan spotted a bit of white paper on the end of a branch.

"This is the place," she said. The men followed the two children as they picked their way down the slope. Bert and Nan pointed out the duffle bag as they passed the tree. It had not been disturbed.

When they drew near the cove, the officers halted. "We'll hide in the bushes here and wait to see what happens." Bert and Nan slipped into a clump of bushes while the policemen settled down in another. They waited silently.

"Isn't this exciting?" Nan whispered to Bert.

He nodded. After a half hour one of the officers came over to the twins. "We're going to scout a little way down the river," he said. "You children stay hidden here. If anyone comes while we're gone just blow on this whistle. It sounds like an owl."

He handed Bert a small clay whistle shaped like an owl's head. Then he and his companion crept silently away among the trees.

Bert and Nan sat quietly for perhaps ten minutes. Then Nan touched Bert's hand. The sound of crackling twigs had broken the silence! Someone was running down the hillside!

CHAPTER XVIII

A LUCKY CAPTURE

"SHALL we blow the whistle?" Nan asked her twin tensely.

"No," Bert whispered. "Let's see who's coming first."

The two waited breathlessly as the plunging footsteps came nearer. Then the bushes parted and a man stepped into the clearing near the shore.

Henry Kraus! Close behind him came John Betz, who was lugging the duffle bag, and the blond, stocky man Bert and Nan had seen talking to Kraus in the Capitol.

The blond man walked to the water line and peered down the river. "See our boat, Smith?" Kraus asked.

As Smith shook his head, Kraus sighed. "The Big Boss is late," he said. "I'll be glad to get out of here and away from those kids! They seemed to be everywhere I went this past week."

"Didn't that black beard fool them?" John Betz asked with a sneer.

"I had good reason for wearing that!" Kraus replied angrily. "The F.B.I. has my record and description from my government job. They might have picked me up if I hadn't disguised myself. And when I wore that pink turban," he continued with pride, "everyone thought I belonged to the Indian Embassy."

"But it didn't fool those kids!"

"I admit they didn't pay any attention to that warning I sent when I returned the girl's camera, or when I crept up behind the young boy in the Wax Museum," Kraus said. "But I got rid of them when I let the air out of their tires!"

"We wouldn't have had all this trouble if Betz had stolen those plans in Lakeport as he was supposed to do!" Smith said bitterly.

"That young kid got in my way. He told Ayler that I had the papers, and I never had a chance to get hold of them again."

"Well, it's all over now," Kraus reminded them. "After the Big Boss shows up we'll soon be out of the country on his ship."

"That's right," Smith said with satisfaction. "We've done the job we were hired to do. Now we can enjoy ourselves in Europe on the money his country pays us!"

Suddenly Bert and Nan heard the putt-putt of

a motor launch. "Somebody's coming!" Nan whispered. "You'd better blow the whistle!"

Bert put the little clay owl's head to his lips. "Who-hoo! Who-hoo!" it called.

"What's that?" Bert asked nervously.

"Relax!" Kraus replied. "We're in the woods, remember? It's an owl!"

At that moment a motor launch rounded the point and made its way into the cove. The three men ran down to greet the short, stocky man at the wheel.

"He's the one who was with Kraus at the embassy!" Bert said in a low voice. "He must be the Big Boss!"

The man threw a line to Kraus, then jumped to the ground. "Let's see those plans before you get on this boat," the skipper said gruffly. "I've had enough trouble with you guys! I'm not letting you double-cross me now!"

Sullenly Kraus opened a brief case which he had been carrying. He pulled out some blue papers and showed them to the skipper.

"Good!" he said. "Get in the boat. Our ship is anchored in Chesapeake Bay, waiting for us."

The three men hurriedly climbed into the launch. Their plan of escape was working!

"Help!" Nan screamed in desperation.

At the sound of her voice the men turned quickly. But before they could do anything, the two Virginia policemen ran into the clearing.

"Halt!" one of them called.

"Come on!" the Big Boss yelled. "Run for it!" Hastily he started the launch and prepared to leave the cove.

But before he could do so, the police launch rounded the point and headed into the cove. The thieves' escape was blocked! A few minutes later the angry criminals were standing on the shore under the watchful eyes of the police.

Freddie and Flossie ran up to the older twins. "Did you find Mr. Ayler's plans?" Freddie asked excitedly.

"The police have them," Nan replied happily.

"Those kids again!" Kraus groaned. "How did they know we had stolen Ayler's drawings?"

"I found the attaché case at the big museum!" Flossie said proudly. "And your fingerprints were all over it!"

Kraus muttered that he had been stupid to leave the case there. He had been sketching some motors and wanted to get rid of it in case he should be stopped by any official.

"I suppose you left your Ronda down by the docks to throw us off the track," Bert remarked.

The man nodded. "But we got the Big Boss out of the way the night we met him at the Lincoln Memorial," he said triumphantly. "We saw you at the Shishkabob and were afraid you'd follow us! That's when we found out where you were staying!"

The thieves' escape was blocked!

"But how did you know we would be out here?" Smith asked in a puzzled tone.

Bert told him about finding the piece of torn paper in Mr. Ankarian's shop and guessing what it meant. "And Nan saw Kraus looking at maps of the Potomac and Chesapeake Bay in the Library of Congress."

By this time the four crooks had been handcuffed. "I'll take care of these men," Officer Webster declared. "You twins can ride back into Washington in the police car. And thank you all for helping us make this lucky capture."

When the four excited children ran into the hotel an hour later they saw Mr. Ayler in the lobby. "We found your plans!" Freddie called out.

The inventor was overjoyed when he heard that the blueprints had been recovered and the thieves caught. "I'm very happy that you children took an interest in the theft," he remarked. "You're excellent detectives!"

"We have to go home tomorrow!" Flossie said sadly. "Are you going to stay here?"

Mr. Ayler said that the men at the Pentagon were very interested in his idea for a space vehicle. "I'm staying for a few more meetings, but I'll see you in Lakeport next week!"

Mrs. Bobbsey was glad to hear that the mystery had been solved. "You've had a very exciting visit to Washington, haven't you?" she remarked as they were flying home to Lakeport the next day. The twins agreed. "I think I'll write about catching Kraus for my essay," Bert decided.

"And I'll tell the story of Miss Pompret's china for mine," Nan declared.

The next morning when the twins walked to school Charlie and Nellie were eagerly waiting on the corner. "Did you get Mr. Ayler's plans?" Charlie called out.

"We sure did!" Bert replied. Then he and Nan told their friends about the capture of the thieves as they were about to escape by boat.

"You Bobbseys have the most exciting things happen to you!" Nellie commented wistfully as they all went into the school building.

That afternoon Nan had arranged with Flossie to pick up the china pieces and take them to Miss Pompret. "I called the library," Nan said. "This is Miss Pompret's day off, and she'll be at home."

Miss Pompret was delighted when she saw the two girls at her door. "Do come in," she urged, "and tell me all about Washington!"

Flossie held out the hatbox. "We've brought you something," she said, trying to look very serious.

"A hat?" Miss Pompret asked in surprise. "You really shouldn't have!"

The girls laughed. "Open it!" Flossie cried.

Carefully Miss Pompret took the lid off the box and lifted the tissue paper. "Oh!" she exclaimed. "My china! *Where* did you find it?"

"Right in this hatbox!" Nan declared.

Before Nan could explain further, the librarian ushered them into her living room. "I think we should use the cream pitcher and sugar bowl right away," she said with a happy smile. "Sit down and I'll get us a hot drink."

In a few minutes she was back with a plate of cookies and the teapot full of hot chocolate.

"It's bee-yoo-ti-ful!" Flossie exclaimed as she looked at the full set of pink-flowered china.

"I'm so glad to have it all together again!" Miss Pompret said. "Now tell me how you found it."

Nan and Flossie related the story of Della and Mr. Ankarian and Mrs. Wellington.

"You're wonderful detectives!" Miss Pompret declared. "I can't thank you enough for finding the china!"

The next Friday morning, at the school assembly, the prizes for the best Washington papers were awarded. Mr. Tetlow made the announcement.

"We have read all the essays very carefully," he began, "and the prize for the best one written by a girl goes to Nellie Parks for her paper on Mount Vernon."

The children applauded as Nellie walked up

to receive her prize of a silver souvenir spoon of Mount Vernon.

"The prize for the best boy's paper goes to Jack Westley for his account of his visit to the Smithsonian Institution," the principal went on.

"I'll bet that's the first prize Jack ever won!" Charlie whispered to Bert as Jack accepted a model airplane.

"We have two additional prizes," Mr. Tetlow continued with a smile. "These essays were not about the sightseeing trips in Washington, but they were so interesting and unusual that the committee decided to award prizes to the writers."

Everyone waited expectantly.

"These prizes go to Nan and Bert Bobbsey for fine accounts of their adventures in the capital city!"

All the students clapped as Bert and Nan made their way to the platform. Nan thanked Mr. Tetlow for the pretty souvenir cup and saucer. Bert beamed at his new penknife with the picture of the Capitol on the case.

When Mrs. Bobbsey heard of the special awards she said, "I've already invited Miss Pompret and Mr. Ayler to Sunday dinner. Now we can make it a real celebration!"

Bert and Dinah had a private meeting Saturday. "I sure will, Bert!" the jolly cook said when he made a suggestion.

On Sunday when the family came to the dinner table there was a small saucerlike vehicle in the center with the tiny figure of a man at the controls.

"It's Mr. Ayler's space rider!" Freddie exclaimed in delight. "Bert made it!"

Everyone admired the boy's work, and Mr. Ayler said it would have an important place in his office.

Dinner was a gay meal. For dessert Dinah passed ice cream and cookies with white frosting and little pink rosebuds on them.

"They're sugar bowls!" Flossie exclaimed when she examined hers.

"We have most everything here, 'cept the man with the black beard!" Freddie announced with a grin.